THE STORY OF
THE LIFE OF JESUS

SALLY PIERSON DILLON

REVIEW AND HERALD® PUBLISHING ASSOCIATION
HAGERSTOWN, MD 21740

The author assumes full responsibility for the accuracy of all facts and
quotations as cited in this book.

This book was
Edited by Gerald Wheeler
Cover designed by Trent Truman
Cover art by Greg and Tim Hildebrandt
Electronic makeup by Shirley M. Bolivar
Typeset: Berkeley Book 12/16

PRINTED IN U.S.A.

09 08 07 06   5 4 3 2

R&H Cataloging Service
Dillon, Sally Pierson, 1959-
        Victory of the warrior king.

        1. Jesus Christ—Biography—Juvenile works.
I. Title.

232.9

ISBN 978-0-8280-1604-9

DEDICATION

To Andrew S and Scotty D,
To Denice G and Rachel A
Especially loved friends of Yeshua's
(and mine, too!)

Main Characters

BIBLICAL	ADDITIONAL

BIBLICAL

ELIZABETH: mother of John the Baptist

ZECHARIAH: father of John the Baptist

MARY: mother of Yeshua

JOHN THE BAPTIST: forerunner of Yeshua

YESHUA: Jesus Christ

MARY MAGDALENE: friend of Yeshua

MARTHA: sister of Mary Magdalene

PONTIUS PILATE: Roman governor of Judea

ADDITIONAL

MARK: recording angel, narrator

LEVI: a Levite's son, his father is a friend of Zechariah and Elizabeth

RACHEL: cousin and best friend of Mary

DAVID: shepherd boy from Bethlehem

SAMUEL: young disciple of John the Baptist

ANTONIA: centurion's daughter from Capernaum

PETRONIUS: Antonia's father's servant

DEBORAH: Antonia's friend, also from Capernaum

THAD: son of a demoniac in Gadara

SARAH: teenager living in Bethany, neighbor of Mary, Martha, and Lazarus

ELIHU: son of Malchus, servant to the High Priest

ANDREW: boy from Nain

JONATHAN: son of David the leper

CLAUDIA: Pilate's wife, friend of Antonia and Petronius

MARK

TEMPLE IN JERUSALEM

y name is Mark. Of course, the Most High has His own name for me. I received the name Mark from a human named Juanita. You may call me Mark; for a creature with only two vocal chords such as yourself, it is easier to pronounce. The Most High has asked me to share some of my recordings with you from the most fascinating event since the creation of this planet. Every angel not specifically assigned other duties hovers close, eager to see every detail and how humans will respond to it.

We know the basics of the plan, and the Most High has revealed them to human prophets, yet we see no indications that earth is preparing for this event. What are they thinking? I've never been able to read the human mind, but I've recorded enough of them that I have a good idea what they're going to do next. The following are my records of humans during these fascinating times.

Levi

"A re we almost there yet?" Levi asked for the umpteenth time.

"No, son," his father answered. "We still have quite a ways yet. Don't you remember?"

"Because of the babies it's been a long time since I've gotten to come with you to Jerusalem."

His father nodded. "Yes, it was difficult for your mother to travel the past three years, but you have three fine healthy sisters, so it was worth missing a few of the festivals, wasn't it?"

Levi wrinkled his nose. "You never miss any of the festivals," he protested.

"Well, of course I can't miss the festivals. I'm a Levite. Levites attend all of the festivals in Jerusalem. We have to help with the work."

"So let me guess which festival it is this time," Levi said, bounding on to another subject. "Is this the Feast of Weeks?"

"No, it's not . . ."

"Don't tell me," his son interrupted, "um, the Festival of Lights?"

"No, you see . . ."

"Purim! I love Purim."

"No," his father sighed. "It's not Purim."

"Passover?"

The father shook his head.

"But it can't be Atonement, because we haven't had the Feast of Trumpets yet. Is it Trumpets?"

"No."

"I'm running out of feasts," the boy complained.

His father laughed. "Levi, we go to Jerusalem for other things too. Once a year I have to do the actual work in the Temple."

"Inside the Temple?" his son asked in wonder. "You mean farther in than the court of women, where I have been?"

"Yes," his father replied proudly. "The Levites are divided into 24 clans. We each serve one week at a time in the Temple."

"What will you do in the Temple?"

"Once I get there we draw lots to determine our assignments. I might serve as a guard, doorkeeper, musician, or as a Temple servant in some other capacity."

"Can you go anywhere? Can you go into the Most Holy Place and see where God lives?"

"No. If any of us Levites went in there, we would die. We aren't even allowed to approach the altar of sacrifice. That is reserved for the priests. There are 24 clans of them, too, and they each take a week and serve in the Temple too. But they light the altar fires, take care of the offerings of incense and unleavened bread, and kill the sacrificial animals."

"Oh. How come you're not a priest? You're from Levi's family, just like the priests are?"

"Yes, but Levi had a big family. The clans of priests are descendants of Aaron. We are descendants of Moses."

The boy thought a moment. "Since Moses was more important than Aaron, then we should be more important than the priests, right?"

Father laughed. "It doesn't work quite that way, Levi. But everyone is important in God's eyes."

"Even me?"

His father laughed. "Yes, even you."

I smiled. How young these humans start jostling for rank and trying to determine each other's value in God's eyes. Levi was not the first and certainly would not be the last, nor the most vocal, in this pursuit. I shook my head. Humans remain the same from age to age. Thankfully the Almighty alters even less. If these humans just understood how much He loves them and how that never changes no matter what happens, it would give them great security.

Levi slowed his pace, lagging behind the men until his mother and her friends caught up with him. They always traveled to Jerusalem in groups. It was safer that way. The terrain was rugged, and they needed to camp overnight on the way. And bandits, to say nothing of Roman soldiers, lurked along the roads.

The boy spat in the dirt as he thought about them. Everyone hated the Romans. They were always bossing people around, and horrible things happened to anyone who didn't obey them. Levi noticed his mother sitting on some boulders beside the path with her friend Elizabeth. He headed toward them.

"I am so tired," Elizabeth said, pulling off her sandal and rubbing one of her dusty feet. "Every year it gets harder and harder to haul these old bones all the way to Jerusalem. The festivals are wonderful once I get there and I'm always so glad I came, but getting there . . ." She groaned.

Levi's mother nodded. "I know what you mean. I haven't been for three years because the babies were little. But I've really missed it."

Elizabeth looked longingly at the two toddlers and the infant in the woman's arms. "Yes, but children are such a blessing of the Lord. I wouldn't mind missing the festivals if it meant having a child."

Staring at the ground, Levi's mother said nothing. The boy glanced at Elizabeth in confusion. Maybe the woman had meant a grandchild. Elizabeth was way too old to be a mother. Anyone could tell by looking that she was a grandmother-type person.

His confusion was understandable, for both Elizabeth and her husband were elderly and most people were grandparents by their age. Yet the Almighty had not blessed them with any children. It was a great sadness to her and her husband, Zechariah, for everyone viewed the lack of children as a punishment from God. Later that night as they were camping, Levi heard his mother and father whispering in the darkness.

"Poor Elizabeth. She was looking so longingly at the babies. It made me want to just give her one except I wouldn't ever be able to give up any of these."

Levi heard the low mumble of his father's voice, and then Mama said, "It's so hard to understand. After all, Elizabeth is also of the direct line of Aaron. She and Zechariah are godly people, and with such pure lineage, it's hard to understand why the Lord is punishing them in this way."

Now Father's voice was a little louder. Levi raised up on one elbow so he could hear better. "The Lord isn't punishing Zechariah. A good man, he was like a father to me when my own father died so young. He helped my mother. Widows have a hard time, and he taught me the things that my father would have, if he had been alive. God can't be punishing Zechariah. It must be Elizabeth, but the old man does love her. Most men would have taken a second wife or a concubine by now to have children. But yet he has clung to his one wife all these years, even though she has no children."

Mother sighed. "Well, God may have deprived her of children, but every woman dreams of a man who would love her that much."

"I guess so," her husband said. "Especially when he could have taken another, or legally divorced her. She must feel truly cherished."

Levi nodded in the darkness. That was one thing that was obvious to everyone. "I hope," he mumbled to himself, "when I am a really old man like Zechariah, that I will have a wife like Elizabeth and we will love each other just as much." Then the boy laid his head in the crook of his arm and fell asleep.

As the pilgrims reached the crest of the hill, Levi caught his breath in wonder. Squinting, he raised his hand to shield his eyes.

Zechariah laughed. "Yes, young one, that is the impression everyone has when they see the Temple for the first time or after a long absence. Isn't it magnificent!"

"The brightness hurts my eyes," Levi said.

Zechariah nodded his gray head. "Yes, mine, too," he said. "But I just can't tear my eyes away from it. It glows with God's glory."

"It glows with the glory of Herod's white stone," Mother muttered under her breath as Zechariah looked over his shoulder at her but said nothing. All of a sudden the journey did not seem so long. Everyone's steps quickened as they hurried toward the beautiful Temple.

"What's that?" Levi asked, pointing to a huge stone fortress. "It's right up against the Temple. What is it?"

"That," said Father, "is the Antonia fortress. The Romans watch everything from it."

"How dare they build it right next to the Temple so that they can peer down into the very courtyards of it," the boy exclaimed. His father nodded and said nothing.

"As we near the city now," Zechariah said, "we must make no more comments about the Romans."

The boy nodded. He knew it didn't take much to antagonize the Romans, and they could be cruel. "Just pray for the arrival of the Messiah," Zechariah said. Levi understood what he meant. When the Messiah came, the Romans would no longer rule. He whispered a prayer as they walked along.

I watched him intently. For 11 years old he was devout, but his expectations of the coming Messiah, though shared by most in Israel, only set him up for disappointment. I wondered how and when we would be allowed to reveal to him the Messiah's real role. For now, though, I would have to watch and wait, just like Levi and his family and Zechariah and Elizabeth.

The little group of pilgrims soon found their quarters within the city. The women began to settle their few belongings and get ready for an evening meal. Father and Zechariah, with the other men in the group, rounded up their livestock.

"Come here, baby," Levi called to the best lamb from their flock, scooping it up in his arms. He had brought her to offer her as a sacrifice to God. "It's almost time for you to go to the Temple."

Holding her close, he scratched her woolly head. It was hard to think about her being burned on the altar, yet Zechariah had explained to him how God is a God of mercy and how the priests had been taught just the proper way to slit the throat of the animals so that they felt no pain. He hugged the animal so tightly that she grunted. "You won't feel a thing," he said. "I promise. Zechariah promised. It's such an honor, you know, being the most perfect lamb in the whole flock. You are the only one good enough to offer to Yahweh." The lamb bleated as if it understood.

Soon the men were ready. "It's time," Levi said, and he and the lamb followed them toward the Temple. The closer they got, the more enormous and impressive it seemed.

They passed through the gates into the crowded courtyard. Vendors sold sacrificial lambs for those who had not brought one, or whose lambs were not perfect. Only perfect lambs could be sacrificed to God. Money changers sat at their tables, for everyone had to exchange their money for Temple currency. Levi studied the fascinating people—Persians and Babylonians and Greeks who had all come to the Temple.

"Over here, Levi," Father called. A priest stood near the lamb vendors. "Bring your lamb over here. We have to have it inspected."

Levi nodded and presented the lamb proudly. The priest handled her roughly, picking her up and looking at her belly and her legs, then squeezing her back leg hard. The animal bleated in surprise and pain.

"He's hurting her," the boy hissed.

"I'm afraid this lamb is lame," the priest announced. "Only perfect lambs are acceptable for sacrifice. You can't use this one."

"It is the best of our flock," Father protested. "It is perfect."

The priest dropped the animal onto the cobblestones. It limped over to Levi and tried to hide behind his legs.

"It looks like it limps to me," the priest insisted. "The animal may be good enough for whatever village you people come from, but it's not good enough for the Temple—or God. If I were you, I would see what I could get for her at the stall over there and buy one of their lambs. They have good lambs."

Father's fists were clenched at his side and Zechariah's eyes blazed with fury. Levi's throat choked. He didn't want to sacrifice the lamb, but how dare anybody say she wasn't perfect. "It wasn't that way before that priest hurt her leg," he muttered.

Father nodded and made a slight gesture with his hand that Levi knew meant "Don't say anything else right now." The boy fell silent. The sheep vendor said the same thing as the priest and tossed a small coin to Father. "This is all I can give you for a lame one," he said. "Now, how about buying one of our good lambs?"

"How much?" Father asked resignedly. And as the merchant quoted a price, Father's fists clenched again. "That's three times what a lamb is even worth, and more than three times what you gave me for this one."

"Well, it's like the priest said," the vendor replied with a shrug. Father's jaw clenched tightly. He flung the coins down on the table and roughly grabbed the perfect lamb.

I watched carefully as the three prepared to go to the Temple. They had risen before dawn, eaten a quick breakfast, and bathed and dressed with care. Zechariah, to draw lots and find what his tasks would be for the day within the Temple; Levi's father, to find out what his responsibilities would be around the Temple grounds; and Levi, to watch and absorb it all.

"Do you think I'll be able to see you where you're working, Father?" he asked.

"I don't know, Levi. It depends what they assign me, but if you stand close to the doorway you should be able to see."

"I can't wait till next year when I become a son of the law and can enter the courtyard," Levi said wistfully. Being 11, he could only approach as close as the court of women.

"Well, it could be worse," Father said. "You could be a Gentile; then you wouldn't even be allowed in the court of women."

The boy remembered seeing the signs warning that any Gentiles who passed from the outer court into the court of women would pay with their lives.

"Yes," he said, "I'm very thankful I'm not a Gentile, but I'm glad I'm not a woman, too, because at least I'll be a man someday."

Father and Zechariah laughed. Mother and Elizabeth just glanced at each other and said nothing.

Approaching the Temple at sunrise struck awe and reverence into their hearts, just as it had the day before. Father and Levi placed themselves on either side of the elderly priest and helped Zechariah up the long stairway.

"Why do they put in so many steps?" Levi puffed.

Zechariah was too short of breath to answer, but Father replied, "It's to give us reverence, to remind everyone that the Lord is high and lifted up, and so that people outside can't see into the Temple."

"When God gave Moses the plans for the tabernacle in the wilderness, did He have stairs in it?" Levi asked. Zechariah shook his head, breathing heavily. The boy began thinking to himself.

It made me think too. The Creator I knew had designed the wilderness tabernacle with the specific purpose of being *with* His people, not distancing Himself from them. The steps were a human idea designed to create awe and distance between the Almighty and those He was trying so hard to be with.

As they paused at the top of the steps before entering the court of women, the father turned to his son. "You would have liked Moses' tabernacle, Levi," he said. "I believe families came there. Fathers would bring the sin offering. One could pass through its gates with singing and stand before the altar of sacrifice and watch their sin offering being prepared. There was no court of women, so you would have been allowed to see what was going on."

Levi caught his breath wistfully. "Oh, I wish I had lived back then," he murmured. "Why do we have it like this now? Is this what God wants?"

Zechariah gave him a sharp look. "Levi," hissed his father. "Never question the Temple."

"But . . . but isn't the Temple just a place, and isn't it God's place? Shouldn't we do things the way He wanted it?" Father shot him another warning glance, and Levi fell silent. But he still wondered.

I smiled to myself. This child may not be old enough to become a son of the law until next year, but he thinks, a trait the Almighty takes great delight in.

Levi stood as close to the opening between the court of women and the outer court of the Temple as possible. He watched the priests and the Levites divide into two groups. The priests stood in a semicircle. One of them seemed to be the leader, or the chief, and he was talking. Levi wished he could hear what he was saying. Then all the priests held up their fingers. Some held up just one, some more. The chief priest began counting off until he reached some number he must have decided in his head earlier. The priest he stopped at seemed very excited and stepped back from the group.

The chief priest began to count again, and soon he paused at another, who also bowed and stepped back from the group. After a few moments he had selected four priests. The rest of the group dispersed to other duties. Zechariah walked back toward Levi.

"They didn't pick you for anything?" the boy asked.

"Not this time." Zechariah took a deep breath and smiled. "They will cast lots again for the evening prayers, and there's always tomorrow. I'm serving here all week."

The old priest would have more chances, Levi told himself. "What kind of jobs were the priests who were chosen going to do?" he questioned.

"Ah," said Zechariah. "The first one received the task of cleansing the altar of burnt offering and then preparing the sacrifice."

"That sounds like hard work."

"Yes," said Zechariah, "but what an honor to do that for the Lord."

That it would be, the boy decided. He would never be able to do that, being just a Levite. "What is the second priest going to do?" he continued after some thought.

"The second priest actually offers the sacrifice, and he will also cleanse the candlestick and the altar of incense."

Levi drew in his breath. How wonderful! That meant the priest would be able to enter the holy place, for that was where the candlestick and the altar of incense stood, right before the curtain that separated it from the Most Holy Place. It was as close to God as any Israelite could ever go except for the high priest on the Day of Atonement.

"And the third priest?"

"The third priest will offer incense this morning" Zechariah explained. "It's the most important job for any priest this week."

Levi smiled. So close to the Most Holy Place, and not cleaning, either, but offering incense, making a wonderful fragrance before the Lord while presenting prayers for the Messiah to come. Then he would watch the smoke from the incense gently wafting up from the altar and slipping over the curtain into God's very presence.

"So the fourth priest must have felt a little disappointed by the time he was chosen," Levi observed.

Zechariah shook his head. "All of us are honored to serve God wherever we are asked. I suppose some would consider it is less of an honor to be the fourth one chosen, though he will burn the pieces of the sacrifice on the altar and perform the concluding part of the service. But anything done for God, whether it is in His Temple, before the curtain at the altar of incense, or whether it is chores done at home as a service unto the Lord, is just as important in the eyes of the Almighty."

I nodded until I realized neither of them could see me and weren't even aware I was there, yet I too smiled. The old man was wise and understood many things. And I was glad he was sharing his wisdom with young Levi.

The afternoon seemed to speed by to Levi. Zechariah sat with him as they watched the activities in the Temple. The elderly priest explained each sacrifice as it took place while they peered in through the open gate. It seemed like no time at all until the priests began to assemble in the courtyard again.

"I need to join them," Zechariah told the boy.

"Why, what are they doing?"

"They will be casting lots for the evening burning of the incense."

"But what about those priests over there?" Levi pointed.

"Ah, one can have this honor only once in their life. Those are priests who have already burned incense before the Lord. It was the greatest moment of their life. Never again will they experience anything as wonderful as that. I have never done it. Now I need to go."

Levi nodded. He stood on his tiptoes, watching with anticipation as the casting of lots took place. Suddenly he shrieked with delight, causing a murmur to ripple through the crowds and people to turn and stare at him. But he couldn't help it. They had selected Zechariah.

The old priest turned and faced the entrance of the Temple. He seemed to stand taller, his shoulders less bent, his step firmer. Zechariah gestured to two priests next to him, who flanked him on either side as they walked to the entrance and stepped into the holy place. Levi knew what would come next. Zechariah had explained it all to him. One of the two priests with him would remove the old coals from the altar. The second would lay new coals on it, then they would respectfully back out of the holy place, leaving the chosen priest before the Lord. The third priest would lay the incense on the altar and pray fervently for the coming of the Messiah as the beautiful cloud of smoke arose from the incense and filled the holy place and passed over the veil into the Most Holy Place. His prayers would go right to the mercy seat, the throne of God. Surely God would listen when Zechariah pleaded for the Messiah to come!

The crowd waited. It didn't take long for the prayer and no one was dismissed from the evening worship until the priest offering the incense returned to the entrance of the Temple, raised both hands, and blessed them.

What was taking Zechariah so long? Levi thought to himself. Of course, sometimes old men were a little bit slower. The crowd continued to wait in silence. After what seemed like forever, murmuring broke out. "What has happened? Has the old man become ill in there? He was too old to be given such an important duty." "No, there was nothing physically wrong with him. He's just old—we should respect him, let him take his time. Perhaps he is praying longer for the Messiah. The Almighty knows we need Him now."

Levi tried to shut out the noise of the crowd about him. He remembered the conversation he and Zechariah had had that afternoon. "This would be the perfect time for the Messiah to come," the priest had told him. "Although we hate the Romans with every fiber of our being, they do give us some advantages. We are at the crossroads of the known world right now. Everyone understands common languages all around the world. The Romans have built roads everywhere, and it is easier than it has ever been since the dawn of time for people and messages to travel. If the Messiah were to come now, word could spread everywhere more quickly than we had ever dreamed possible. And surely there has been no time when we have needed Him more than now."

A murmur rippled through the crowd again, startling Levi out of his thoughts. Zechariah had appeared in the doorway. "Thank You, God," Levi whispered. It had been so long. What had Zechariah been doing in there? As Levi struggled to get a better look, he was startled by Zechariah's face. It glowed with such a brightness. The crowd caught its collective breath. "It's like Moses! He has the radiance of Moses!" The whispers spread like wildfire.

When Moses had spoken with God on the mountain, his face had glowed like this. The crowd waited expectantly for Zechariah to raise his hands in benediction and dismiss them. Instead he seemed to be trying to speak and gesturing with just one hand. "We can't hear you. Speak up," someone shouted.

A pain, almost physical, stabbed through Levi as he realized Zechariah was gesturing with his hand because he didn't seem able to speak. He was trying, but he couldn't. Was he able to lift his other hand? Why couldn't he talk?

His two priest friends who had assisted him at the altar of incense rushed to his side. Everyone began trying to understand what he was attempting to communicate. "What happened?" they asked. "Are you ill?" Zechariah continued to gesture wildly. "Did you see something? Did the Lord speak to you? Surely not a demon in the holy place. Was it an angel?"

The more questions they asked, the more frenzied Zechariah's gestures became. Gently they led him off to the side. Another priest blessed the people and dismissed them. Levi could hardly stand it. He wanted to rush into the courtyard up to the entrance of the Temple and help the old man, but he could not go past the portals of the court of women. The priests summoned Levi's father, who led Zechariah gently toward the exit. Another priest sent a servant to bring a donkey to the outer courts. Gently they helped Zechariah onto the donkey, and supporting him on both sides, led him home.

I glided along with them, as shocked as they were, but for different reasons. For I had seen what had happened in the holy place. And I was astounded. Zechariah had been praying for the coming of the Messiah, and Gabriel, our captain, the highest ranking angel in heaven, had appeared before him at the altar and told him that his prayers were being answered. And that the Messiah was coming soon. Even more than that, he notified Zechariah that he and Elizabeth would have a son who would prepare the way for the Messiah.

That had not surprised me, for all of us knew it was almost time, and were watching intently to see what would happen. What was shocking was his disbelief! This human had spent his entire life praying fervently for one thing. And when told his prayers were answered, he responded, not with joy and shouts of celebration and praise, but with disbelief! Humans were impossible to understand. Yet the Almighty and the Creator had such a passionate love for them. I shrugged, grateful that my duties did not include understanding humans, merely recording their activities and responses. Had I been required to understand them, too, I surely would have been judged incompetent.

At home, Levi and his father lifted Zechariah from the donkey and supported him into the house they were staying at for the week. Mother and Elizabeth anxiously rushed to the door. "What happened?" Mother demanded. "Is he OK?"

Zechariah pulled his arms free and flung them around Elizabeth. The two stood there holding each other tightly, rocking back and forth. Tears poured down both of their faces. Elizabeth buried her face in Zechariah's beard. His face still glowed like in the stories of Moses when he had been speaking to God.

"Something happened at the Temple," Father said at last. "Zechariah was chosen to burn incense for the evening prayers. He did not come out for a long time. We were very worried about him.

When he did return he glowed like this," he pointed toward the elderly man. "But he seemed unable to speak. Some of us believe he must have heard from God or at least spoken with an angel. Yet why would he have been stricken speechless?

"In the outer courts was a servant who had studied under a Greek physician. He said this problem was common with people who had had an injury to their head, that often they would be weak on one side and unable to speak for a time. Sometimes they recover, sometimes they die."

Elizabeth drew herself to her full height and her eyes blazed as she snapped, "There is nothing wrong with my husband's head. He has obviously heard from the Lord. Look at his face. How can you deny it? There will always be people who try to explain the Lord's actions with natural explanations as an excuse not to have to believe."

Suddenly she turned pale, took two steps backward, turned on her heel, and walked quickly from the room toward the water jar in the courtyard. She sank to the ground next to it as she took several long slow sips from a cup. Mother frowned. Levi was confused. Did Elizabeth know something that the rest of them had missed? Sometimes old couples seemed to know each other so well they could finish each other's sentences. *Perhaps Elizabeth knows what happened,* Levi thought. *I sure wish I did, and I hope Zechariah is going to be all right. And what is wrong with Elizabeth?*

He wandered back toward the stables. "I will take the donkey back," he offered as his father laid his hand on his shoulder.

"Good. I'll go with you." They walked along in silence.

"Do you have any idea what happened in there?" the boy asked.

His father shook his head. "No son, but Zechariah was in there praying for the coming of the Messiah, and from the glow on his face, my feeling is that something wonderful is going to happen. Let's both continue to pray for that."

Levi nodded. "Oh yes, I certainly will."

Father and son both prayed silently as they walked along together with the oblivious donkey. A peace settled over the two. Levi drew a deep breath and let it out. Whatever had happened to Zechariah, Yahweh, the King of the universe, was in control. He had heard Zechariah's prayers and everything was going to be all right, no matter how He chose to answer.

RACHEL

NAZARETH

 must admit that when I received the assignment to record Rachel and her choices in Nazareth, I felt a twinge of disappointment. It was so close to the time for the birth of the Messiah. I knew from the prophecies that it would take place in Bethlehem, yet I had been sent to a tiny town with a bad reputation instead. However, the Mighty One had always been good to me, and His assignments were always reasonable and fair, so I swallowed my disappointment and prepared to record for Rachel. At least I had not had to go to some obscure village on a continent far away. I would still be able to watch as the Almighty's secret plan unfolded.

Nazareth seemed to be a town with a definite seedy side, though a few families still worshiped the Almighty, Rachel's family being one of them. She was a devout Hebrew girl who, having just stepped across the threshold from childhood to young woman-hood, was available for marriage.

Rachel ran down the path toward the village well. Her friend, Mary, was already there in line with the other women to draw water. She grabbed Mary's arm and whispered, "It's happened! It's started!"

Mary flung her arms around Rachel. "Now we can both be married women together!"

The other girl nodded. "I hope they choose someone really wonderful for me," she said.

"Of course they will," Mary said with a smile. "They love you."

Suddenly Rachel's face clouded. "A lot of people we know have families that love them, but they picked old men for them because those men were rich." Her friend looked at the ground. "Oh, I'm sorry, Mary; I didn't mean you. Anyway, Joseph isn't that old—I mean really really old."

"Joseph is quite a bit older than I am," Mary replied. "But he's a good man, and he needs a mother for his children."

"Yes, and I know he will be really good to you. Joseph is a very kind man. Yet I would really like somebody closer to my age. I think it would be easier to be a first wife." Mary shyly nodded and blushed. "But I know you'll really be happy with Joseph. Still, isn't this exciting! We might end up getting married at the same time! Who knows?"

"It's possible," Mary replied. "I've been betrothed for only a short time."

"Do you know when Joseph is going to take you to his home?"

Mary laughed. "Oh, only the bridegroom's father knows that for sure. If it was up to our grooms, they would barely construct the shell of a room before they would move us in. It's a good thing it's left up to the fathers. Joseph's family will make sure that he builds a nice room and completes it. Perhaps with a nice table and a storage trunk."

"Yes, those things would be nice," Rachel agreed. "And it's good that Joseph is preparing you a room of your own."

"With children already," Mary added, "it will be good to have two rooms for all of us. Besides, I would always feel as if I was in Hadassah's room, even though she's been dead for a long time now."

"I know what you mean," Rachel said. "It would feel strange."

By this time the group of older women had drawn their water, and the two girls were able to approach the well.

I followed them as they carried their heavy water pots up the dusty street to their homes. Negotiations for marriages took place early in this culture. Though Rachel was only 12 years of age, it was not an unusual time to get married. Her betrothal would usually last about a year. The girls, in their enthusiasm, had chatted about their prospective husbands needing the time to finish adding a room for them onto the family home that usually surrounded a common court-yard area. Another reason for the year-long wait was to make sure that the young bride was not carrying someone else's child. Surely, with these two worshipers of Jehovah, that would not be a problem.

As they walked along, Rachel's face saddened again. "During the negotiations for your betrothal, did you ever feel like you were being sold to the highest bidder?"

Mary laughed. "A little bit, though I don't think I got sold to the highest bidder, because I believe Cleophas actually offered more money. I think my father felt Joseph would be a better husband."

"Yes," Rachel agreed, "Joseph will be a good husband."

"Anyway, a lot of the money that your future husband gives your father for a dowry is going into coins for your headpiece. You'll get to keep it if you're ever widowed or divorced. Fathers retain only a small amount of that as compensation for the loss of all the work we do. And since men don't think that's worth much, most of it will be yours anyway."

Rachel laughed. "That's true; I hadn't thought of it like that."

"It will be OK," Mary said, "really it will. You're just having jit-ters over the idea of becoming betrothed. It made me nervous too, but once that is over, you have a long time yet to get used to the idea before you will actually move into his house."

Rachel sighed. "You always make me feel better, Mary."

Her words made me smile. The Almighty always planned for His children to support each other with their friendships. Humans without close friendships have to bear their trials and anxieties alone, and the burden is much heavier because of that.

I watched Rachel as she carried the water back to her house and helped her mother prepare for the special dinner that evening. They baked fresh bread, brought out their best dried fruit so carefully prepared earlier that year, and sent Joshua, her little brother, out to choose a chicken and have it butchered and blessed by the rabbi. The time seemed both to drag and rush by at the same time. Her stomach had twisted into a tight knot by the time Judah and his father, Matthew, arrived at the house.

Rachel's mind was in a blur as they did all the formal greetings. She could hardly eat. Judah seemed nervous too. He spent a lot of time looking at his plate. He did sneak a shy glance at her. She smiled and then they both looked down, embarrassed.

"And now," her father said, turning to Matthew and to Judah, "for the business at hand."

Judah reached into the bag he had brought and produced a pouch of coins. "The bride price we agreed on," he said, and passed it to Rachel's father.

"The price is paid," he said, placing the coins on the table before him.

The two fathers talked for several minutes and then Matthew and Judah prepared to leave. Before Judah slipped out the door, he stepped over next to Rachel and whispered, "I'm going home now to prepare a special place for you, but the next time I come back, I'm taking you with me, and then you and I will always be together as long as we live."

Rachel's heart jumped into her throat. She lifted her eyes and stared into his face, and he smiled at her. "Judah," his father said, "come on, we must be going. It's not seemly for you to stand chatting with young women not of your family."

Judah turned and smiled at Matthew. "But Father, I wasn't. I was just talking with my wife."

The whole family laughed. Rachel drew a deep breath. *What a lovely sound, "my wife,"* she thought. She hoped it wouldn't be long before Judah took her to his home.

The next day, on the way to the well, Rachel and Mary were whispering and giggling together as usual. Mary caught her friend's arm. "Do you realize, now we're both married women?"

Rachel laughed. "It doesn't feel much different than before, does it?"

"No. I suppose that's because we haven't gone to live in the homes of our husbands. Still, it sounds kind of exciting to say 'husband,' doesn't it?"

"It's true," Rachel giggled, "but even though we haven't gone to live with them or borne their children, if something were to happen to them, we would be widows."

That thought left both of them sober.

"What's the matter with you?" asked Mahitobel, a neighbor woman. "You look miserable on a day when at least one of you should be really happy." She winked at Rachel. Both girls looked up.

"We were just thinking that if something happened to our men, it would make us widows.

The older woman laughed. "Well, if anything does happen to any of our men, we would be left widows, but all of us will be widows someday, unless we die first—and that would be worse." The girls nodded, thinking of all of the women who had died in childbirth in Nazareth. "Since it's going to happen to all of us eventually," she continued, "I don't worry about it. After all, this is the day the Lord has made, and I will rejoice and be glad in it."

Human life was short. So many of the people of this time would be dead by the time they were in their late 20s. Few lived beyond 40 human years. But the Almighty never intended for them to spend the time they had worrying about their demise. They had people to love and much to rejoice in.

Some weeks later Rachel sat on the stones next to the well, waiting. Where was Mary? The girls looked forward to their daily chats at the well in the cool of the morning. Finally, Rachel looked up to see her friend's mother walking briskly to the well with the family water pot.

"Where's Mary?" asked Rachel.

"She's ill," the woman answered abruptly.

"Oh, what's the matter? May I come visit her?"

"No, she has a fever. She needs to rest."

"Well, tell her I hope she feels better."

Mary's mother looked and met Rachel's direct gaze. "So do I," she said. "So do I."

During the following two days Mary's mother continued to draw the water for the family. On the third night the weather was hot as families all slept up on the flat roofs of their homes, where they could get a little evening breeze. All the guardian angels were in their places for night duty except Rachel's. The girl, after waiting until everyone's even breathing and soft snoring told her they were resting quietly, had slipped down the side stairs and hurried through the narrow and crooked street.

Her guardian and I followed closely. Nazareth was hardly a safe place for a young girl to be out alone in the daytime, much less at night. Standing beneath the fig tree outside Mary's house, she gave a low whistle. After repeating it, she heard one back from the roof of Mary's house. Soon Mary, her guardian, and her recorder slipped down the stairs and out to the tree.

The two girls embraced tearfully. "Mary, what's wrong? I was so worried about you. I've missed you so much. Are you well?"

Her friend nodded.

"But your mother said you were ill."

Mary sighed. "Mother thinks I am ill."

"Well, what happened?"

"You have to promise to believe me," Mary began.

Puzzled, Rachel answered, "Of course I'll believe you. I've never known you to tell a lie in your whole life. What is the matter?"

Mary tried to smile. "Well, if you do believe me, you'll be the first. Something happened. An angel appeared to me."

Rachel gasped. "An angel?"

"Quiet," Mary whispered. "You're going to wake the whole family."

"I'm sorry. An angel?"

"Yes. The angel told me that I am to have a child and that He will save His people from their sins."

Even in the dim light of the stars Mary could see excitement fill Rachel's face. "The Messiah? That's wonderful! Every girl in Israel has prayed and hoped that they would be the mother of the Messiah. What on earth is wrong with that?"

"I'm pregnant now," Mary replied softly.

"You are?" Rachel's eyes widened. "But we always said we were going to wait until after . . ."

Mary grimaced. "I know. But Joseph and I didn't do anything!"

"What do you mean? How can you be pregnant if . . . ?"

"I don't know. I don't know how God does these things, but the angel told me that I am carrying His child. My monthly flows have stopped and, well, I have the other signs too."

Rachel's mouth gaped open. "Mary, you didn't fool around on Joseph, did you?"

Mary stared at her friend in horror. "How could you even think that?"

"I'm—I'm sorry." Rachel thought for a moment. "Are you sure about this angel thing? The angel didn't do anything to you or hurt you, did he?"

"No. He just told me what was going to happen, and I told him it was OK."

"It just doesn't seem right. Why would God bring disgrace on the family that was going to raise the Messiah? You know everyone will think that . . ."

"Yes, I know." Mary bit her lip, fighting back tears. "That's what my parents think now."

"What about Joseph?"

Mary began to cry softly. "Joseph loves me." Rachel could barely hear the words.

"But—Mary, have you told him? If Joseph finds out, he could have you stoned."

The girl cried harder. "He won't have me stoned. He's already been told. I'm to be divorced quietly to avoid a scandal."

"He must really love you," Rachel gasped.

"Yes, he does. I can't understand why doing God's will would bring such sorrow and embarrassment to him. He's a good man."

"You're sure this is God and not some night demon?" Rachel demanded.

Mary struggled for words. "He said something else—that my aunt Elizabeth is also expecting a child and that . . ."

"Your aunt Elizabeth?" Rachel protested incredulously. "Your old aunt Elizabeth, the one that's married to the priest Zechariah?"

Wordlessly Mary nodded. Rachel let out a giggle. "That would *have* to be a sign from God. If your aunt Elizabeth could be pregnant at all, then it wouldn't be hard for anyone to believe you were carrying the Messiah!"

"That's what I'm hoping. I've convinced my parents to let me visit her."

"Now is a good time. That way perhaps it will keep the rumors from circulating, and anybody who wants to stone you has some time to calm down."

"Yes," Mary agreed, "although I cannot believe that a God as powerful as ours would fill me with His Messiah, then allow me to be stoned. Surely He already has a plan in mind."

Rachel hugged her. "You've always had so much more faith than me."

Her friend dried her tears on her sleeve. "I wish I had more right now. Sometimes I'm so sure, and then sometimes I just feel so sad. I find myself crying for no reason."

To her own surprise Rachel suddenly laughed. "Isn't that supposed to be a sign of pregnancy, Mary?"

Mary managed to laugh too. "Yes, I suppose it is. I'm to leave tomorrow early. I just have to find out how Elizabeth is. It will answer so many questions."

Rachel hugged her. "I'm so sorry you and Joseph are getting divorced. I don't understand it at all, but they do say God does mysterious things."

Swallowing hard, Mary replied, "Well, this will go down in history as one of the most mysterious. I'm sure of it."

The two girls hugged again and then Rachel slipped away toward home, and Mary slowly climbed the steps.

The two girls may have been in tears, but an ecstasy filled me that I had only felt during some of our greatest praise sessions in the presence of the Almighty. It made me want to fly spinning spirals through earth's atmosphere shouting praises to the Mighty One! How could I have been disappointed at being sent to Nazareth? I had been given an assignment close to the very place where the Creator was to become human. In fact, He was right in my presence—in the body of this young girl!

The other guardians were as excited as I was. We made sure

to keep our shouts of praise only on frequencies that would not disturb human ears. What an honor! And we wondered how Mary would wind up in Bethlehem as the prophecies had stated. But it wasn't a problem. The Almighty had handled much more difficult geography than that, and we were certain that everything would work out. All of us just hoped that we would be assigned there too.

RACHEL

NAZARETH, SEVERAL MONTHS LATER

awn was barely streaking the sky when Rachel's guardian prodded her awake. The girl yawned and stretched. Going to the well was no fun anymore since Mary had left. She often rose early to draw water before the crowds came. The happy chatter of the other women just made her feel her loneliness even more keenly. Grabbing the family's heavy water pot, she headed for the well. In the dim light she thought she saw a figure sitting on the low wall next to the well. Could it be?

"Mary!" she shrieked, and, dropping her water jar, she went flying toward her friend. The other girl jumped up and flung her arms around Rachel.

"I'm so glad to see you! When did you come back? This is wonderful."

Mary laughed. "I got back last night. It was late and I haven't slept much, but I thought I'd come early in case I could catch you before the others got here."

"Oh, I'm so glad to see you," Rachel sputtered. "Tell me everything. What happened? And, and are you still . . . I mean, were you really . . . ?"

"I am." Mary pulled her garment tightly against her body to reveal that her stomach was beginning to swell with child.

"Does . . . are you divorced? What has Joseph said?"

"It's all wonderful," Mary exclaimed. "God has worked everything out. Aunt Elizabeth really is pregnant. She will be having her baby any day now."

"Really?" said Rachel breathlessly. "Then it's true?"

Mary nodded. "It's true. And an angel came to Joseph in a dream and told him that I had been telling the truth and that he shouldn't be afraid to keep me as his wife."

"So you're going to be married?"

"We are married," said Mary. "There won't be any big wedding celebration, since—well, you can almost see now."

Rachel stood back and looked at her friend's figure. "People might not be able to tell the difference between this and your having eaten a lot at aunt Elizabeth's house."

"I considered that too," laughed Mary, "but my condition will be unmistakable soon enough."

"So what did Joseph say?"

Mary smiled. "He's so wonderful. Arriving at Aunt Elizabeth's house, he said he had come to fetch his wife home. Aunt Elizabeth didn't really want to let me go, but Joseph was insistent, and since we had not been divorced yet, I am his wife. So he brought me home to his house. He said that if the Almighty was going to send His Messiah to be born through his wife, the least he could do was protect the two of them, and it is his intention to take very good care of us."

"Oh, how sweet," Rachel sighed.

"And then, as Aunt Elizabeth was sputtering about not letting me leave, he stopped and whispered to her that he didn't think it fitting or proper for a virgin to be in the house when a child was being born. You should have seen the look on Aunt Elizabeth's face."

Mary and Rachel rocked with laughter. "Well, it's true," Mary said. "I may be pregnant, but I am still a virgin." Rachel nodded. "Aunt Elizabeth didn't say another word. She just helped me get my things together and packed us a huge lunch basket to take with us. I'm going to miss her so much."

"I'll bet she'll miss you too."

"Yes, but I'm really happy to be back here, and I'm happy to be in Joseph's home."

"Are you going to tell anyone?" Rachel asked. "I mean, about the Father of your baby?"

Mary shook her head. "Joseph and I talked about it. The angel didn't tell us what to do about other people, so we have decided to say nothing. Joseph said people can think whatever they like, and if they assume this is his child, he'll be proud for them to believe that until God lets us know something different."

"But, they'll think that you two, um . . ."

"Yes, I know," Mary sighed. "But I had a long time to think about that. There have been other times when the things God has asked His people to do haven't always made sense to them at the time. All the stories of the children of Israel in the desert—they thought God had sent them out to starve because there wasn't any food there. It didn't make sense to them and yet God had a plan all along. After enough such experiences you would think they would have learned to trust Him. Now it's happening to me, and I have to trust Him too. This is all He told me, so I just need to trust Him until He tells me what to do next."

"I won't tell anyone either," Rachel said. "No matter what people say."

"Good," Mary replied grimly, "because I imagine they'll be saying lots of things, but likely very little about a Messiah."

Slowly Rachel nodded.

I found myself nodding in agreement along with her. The gossip would be vicious, but their decision to keep the child's parentage a secret was right. The Almighty had chosen well this young woman and her loving carpenter husband. I marveled at His wisdom as once again piece after piece of His plan fell into place. Truly He is amazing.

LEVI

OCTOBER, SMALL TOWN IN JUDEA

other walked into the house and stepped over to the brazier to warm her hands over the coals. "It's a boy," she announced. Levi sat up and rubbed the sleep from his eyes.

"Good for Zechariah!" Father commented.

"Humph," Mother snorted. "Good for Elizabeth, you mean. It was a long hard labor and she's an old woman, yet she bore up well and the child is strong and healthy."

"That's wonderful," Father said, pulling on his outer robe. "Come on, Levi, let's go congratulate Zechariah!"

* * *

Mother had been baking all morning and Father had purchased a gift in the marketplace. Levi could hardly contain his excitement. It was the eighth day after the child's birth, and the infant would be circumcised today. And while the baby might not think highly of that, it would be reason for a party for the rest of the village. They were all invited to Zechariah's and Elizabeth's home to celebrate. It had been traditional to name the child at circumcision ever since Abram and Sarai had received their new names at Abram's circumcision.

"What do you think they'll name him?" Levi asked his father.

"I think they should name him Zechariah."

"Why? It is not common around here for babies to be named after their fathers if their fathers are still living," Levi observed.

"That's true, but Zechariah is an extraordinarily good man, spoken to by God Himself—or at least an angel of God. And it would be an honor for any child to be named after him."

"That's a good idea," his son said. "Too bad Zechariah can't speak. How terrible it must be not to be able to tell people about everything that has happened to you or to name your own baby."

"He can still name the baby. We have the little wax tablets for him to write on with the stylus, so he can still voice his opinion, just not as loudly as you do."

Levi laughed. I laughed too.

The party was magnificent. Levi had eaten until he was sure he could not hold another mouthful. The baby's cries from the circumcision ceremony had quieted, and he too was as full as Levi and snoozing contentedly in his mother's arms. Servants continued to bring trays of food to the already-full tables. And the men gathered around Zechariah, congratulating him and giving name suggestions while the women commented on the baby's size, how much hair he had, how strong and healthy he seemed, and then compared him to their own babies.

Suddenly the other guardians and recorders backed up in respect. Gabriel, the highest ranking angel of our order, had come to the home of Zechariah and Elizabeth. I had heard him speak to Zechariah and strike him dumb in the first place when the priest had expressed disbelief at the thought of having a child when he was so old. In addition, Gabriel had revealed the Almighty's plan to Mary and received her agreement before the Holy Spirit filled her with the Child. Now Gabriel was here at the party. The humans continued their chatter, oblivious to his presence. He stood before Zechariah. Everyone continued suggesting names. "I tell you," Levi's father insisted, "he should be named Zechariah after his father. It would be an honor to any child to carry the name of such a man."

"Yes, yes," the other men echoed. "Zechariah it is. We're all in agreement."

The old priest shook his head and groaned. It could have sounded like "no," but we weren't sure. He started gesturing wildly.

"No, no, don't do that," Levi's father interrupted. "Here, let me get you a writing tablet. You can write it for us."

Someone brought the tablet and pressed the stylus into Zechariah's hand. Carefully he wrote with his shaky hand on the wax surface: "His name is John."

"John?" Levi's father asked incredulously. "John? There's no one in the family named John."

"No, there's not," Zechariah said.

After a moment of silence everyone broke into a babble of amazement. "He spoke. Zechariah is talking!"

"What did he say?"

"Something about John."

"Who's John?"

"The baby."

They fell silent again. "The angel told me," the old man began shakily, and then his voice became stronger and more clear. "The angel told me his name should be John."

The crowd broke into cheers, then fell silent again. Gabriel turned and, saluting the rest of us, left the building. Zechariah seemed almost aware of his presence. Gesturing at the crowd of humans, he said, "I've been so eager to tell you for all these many months. You must listen. The Messiah is coming!"

"Is John the Messiah?" the people asked.

"No, no, no," the old priest protested. "He's the one to prepare the way. My son will be the Elijah we've been waiting for. But the Messiah is coming! He is soon to be born."

The people shouted cheers again. "The Messiah will soon be born. The Messiah! That's wonderful! He'll get rid of these Romans!"

"He's only going to be born," the old priest managed to interrupt. "You have to let Him grow up first."

"But it will happen in our lifetime. This is wonderful."

As the crowd continued to chatter and speculate, Zechariah rose from his seat and moved to where the women were. "Elizabeth," he said. Her jaw dropped in amazement, and she stood.

Turning to her guests, she said, "Please continue with the feast. My husband and I must talk."

Levi smiled as he watched the two of them, cradling their sleeping son between them, walking a distance away where they could speak privately for a few moments. The boy started to follow.

"Come on, Levi," his father called. "Give them some time. They haven't talked in a while—at least not Zechariah. He'll probably be excited to get some words in after all these months with only Elizabeth being able to express her opinion."

RACHEL

achel watched as her friend, Mary, trudged slowly toward the well carrying the family's empty water jar. Her gait was awkward as she tried to walk, leaning backward to balance the weight of her unborn Child as well as the heavy clay vessel. Rachel set her own jar down and rushed over. "Let me carry that for you, Mary. You're getting too big to do this. Can't someone help you?"

"I'm fine," Mary protested. "Really, I can do this. Women have been having babies for thousands of years. I can do this too," but her voice sounded a little shaky.

"Well, I will do it for you today," Rachel said firmly. She set Mary's jar down next to the well as they waited for their turn.

"Mary, you've been growing pretty fast there," one woman snickered. "But don't feel bad. The first one can come anytime. It's after that that they take nine months."

The women all laughed. Mary's face reddened. Her eyes met with Rachel's briefly and then she stared at the ground and said nothing.

"Awe, leave her alone," another woman said. "It's not the first time something like that has happened around here. Give her a break." Soon they were chatting about other things.

Rachel carried Mary's water jar back to where she and Joseph lived with his children and an aging mother. "They can be so heartless," the other girl said when they were out of earshot.

Mary nodded and replied, "Well, Joseph and I have bigger problems than that right now."

"What's the matter?"

"Caesar Augustus."

"Yeah, well, he's a pain in all of our sides," Rachel laughed. "What's new with that?"

"What's new," Mary explained, "is he sent out that decree for all of us to be taxed."

"Yes, I know. None of us can afford his stupid taxes."

"It's not just that. Everyone has to return to their hometown to pay it."

"So?" Rachel said. "That's here, isn't it?"

"Well, for us it used to be. Now I am married to Joseph, and his family came here from Bethlehem. He has to return to Bethlehem to register and pay his taxes there."

"But that's a horribly long trip from here," her friend protested. "You have to either cross Samaria or follow the Jordan Valley. Either way it is a long, rough trip. How are you going to do that? You look like you're ready to give birth any day now."

Mary sighed, then smiled. "But you know what? Remember the prophecy: 'But thou, Bethlehem . . .'"

Rachel caught her breath. "The Messiah! Of course—He's to be born in Bethlehem!" She hugged Mary. "God is going to work things out, just like the prophet said in the first place. Perhaps that was the plan all along." And then she got a gleam in her eye. "Wouldn't old Caesar Augustus be disgusted to know that the God of this ornery little bunch of people in Palestine who he has so much trouble controlling, was using him to work out His plans, instead of the other way around?"

The two girls chortled in merriment, and I joined them, recalling several times when the Almighty had used rulers, pompous with their overgrown egos, to implement His plans and His will on this little planet.

DAVID

avid stared into the crackling fire and yawned. Everyone in his family was tired, for the night before, his mother had given birth to a fine, healthy son. It had prompted great rejoicing, but little sleep. The boy had spent the night running every few hours between the men on the hillside watching the sheep, and his home in the village, checking to see if the child had been born yet. David had not been very old when his sisters had been born and he did not remember the screams and moans that accompanied labor and childbirth. The sounds of his mother's suffering had threatened to rip his heart out of him. Yet now it was all over. He shifted his position and smiled. Another boy in the family! Now he had a brother.

"What are you smiling about?" Jacob, an older herdsman sitting near the bubbling pot of stew, asked him.

The boy shook his head. "Just thinking about my brother," he said proudly.

"Ah yes," the older shepherd sighed. "The birth of every male brings hope to those of us who still believe in the traditions of our ancestors. We long for each one to be more than just another mouth to feed, more than just someone to herd flocks or toil in the fields." The others nodded. "May he be the Consolation of Israel."

The Consolation. It was a word that some used to refer to the Messiah. David smiled. Wouldn't it be wonderful if his little brother was the Messiah! Every woman in Israel hoped her child would be the coming Messiah.

"It *is* possible, isn't it?" David asked after some thought. "We were talking the other night about the prophecies. Don't some expect the Messiah soon?"

Most of the shepherds nodded. "And isn't He supposed to be born here in Bethlehem?" David continued.

Again the other shepherds expressed their agreement. "I don't know," Shemian said slowly throwing some branches into the fire. "Our people have been talking about the Messiah and expecting Him for thousands of years. I wonder if He's any more likely to show up tonight than last night. I think the Consolation is all in our heads." Rumbles of disagreement spread through the small band of shepherds.

"No, I think He should be coming soon," Jacob protested. "I've heard that last year one of the priests in Jerusalem had an angel appear to him and tell him that the Messiah was soon to be born."

"Some claim that he was just a senile old priest who had a stroke while he was on altar duty," Shemian interrupted.

"No, no, I heard he was a good and devout man," someone else protested.

"Well," Shemian replied, "at any rate, he wasn't able even to speak or function normally for months after that—almost a year."

The shepherds started arguing among each other. "Well," David said finally, "whether the priest had a stroke or not, I believe in the Messiah, and I will be glad to see Him."

Shemian fell silent and went back to poking the fire with a stick.

I could hardly contain my excitement as I saw the host of angels gathering on the hillside. Heaven had summoned many from their other duties for this special event. Bursting with their good news, they planned to tell the shepherds that the Messiah was about to arrive.

"Now, don't scare them to death," I admonished them. "Remember, these are humans. They frighten easily."

One angel decided to materialize and allow the shepherds to adjust to his presence before the rest appeared. Even then David and the other shepherds flung themselves with shrieks of terror on the ground, shielding their eyes from his brightness. "Don't be afraid," the angel told them.

I nodded as if to say, "What did I tell you?" It took him several minutes to get them to stop shaking and to listen to what he had to say.

"Your Consolation has arrived," he said. "The Messiah is born!"

The shepherds were too shocked to respond and just gaped at him. "He's in Bethlehem, even now," the angel explained gently to them. "You will find him wrapped in swaddling clothes but lying in a manger."

"A manger?" It sounded as odd to me as it did to the shepherds. Hardly a place to put any baby, much less an infant King. Then the rest of the angels could contain themselves no longer. The entire hillside and sky filled with their glowing forms as they shouted and sang with joy about the birth of the Messiah.

I joined in with the singing, although with my duties, I was not permitted to appear. The other angels were the only beings allowed to manifest themselves tonight, and they wanted to express all their joy and make it a truly spectacular celebration. And it was.

As the light died from the sky and David's eyes became used to the darkness again, he asked his fellow shepherds, "Well, shall we go find Him?"

"Yes, yes," cried the others. Even Shemian, their resident cynic, agreed.

"What about the sheep?" Jacob asked.

"We won't be gone too long. If the Almighty cared enough to send angels to tell us the Messiah is born, I'm sure He will keep our sheep safe."

"Then let's go," David shouted. "Let's find this Baby." In the back of his mind he kept wondering: *Could it be my little brother? But where did they find a manger?* What an honor it would be to have the Messiah for a little brother. The shepherds rushed into the village of Bethlehem.

David stopped by his home. It was dark. Only the coals from the night's fire lay glowing. His sisters, mother, and the tiny baby were sound asleep together on the raised platform in his one-room home. The donkey was tied on the other side. She opened her eyes and glanced at David, then closed them again. No manger. Emerging from the house, he caught up quickly with the rest of his fellow shepherds.

I suppose that was a stupid idea anyway, he thought. *The Messiah would never come from my family.*

By this time one of the shepherds had checked at the inn. No baby born there that night, but the innkeeper recalled a couple looking for somewhere to rest earlier that evening. He had directed them toward the limestone caves on the other side of town where many people stabled their animals, for the inn was full and the couple apparently did not have kin to provide them lodging. The floors in the inn's rooms and even the courtyard were packed with sleeping bodies. The shepherds were familiar with the limestone caves and hurried in that direction.

Sure enough, they spotted a flicker of light in one of the caves. As they approached it, they saw a young girl curled up in the corner, her back resting against a mound of straw and holding a tiny Baby. The Infant was wrapped tightly in swaddling bands, as all healthy babies were. All newborns were bathed and rubbed with salt and then wrapped tightly in swaddling clothes to provide them a sense of security and warmth and to help their limbs grow straight and strong.

The shepherds silently filed into the cave and, without saying a word, knelt before the Baby. Finally Jacob spoke. "It is the Messiah, and we've come to worship Him."

An older man entered the cave. Seeing the rough shepherds, he looked alarmed, but the young mother smiled at him. He stood by her protectively. "They've come to worship Him, Joseph," she said.

The husband stared as the shepherds bowed their heads. Mary turned and lay the Baby back in the manger. "His name is Yeshua," she told them.

The shepherds nodded. The name meant "the Lord is salvation." It was a common Hebrew name, but a good one for the Messiah. The shepherds remained on their knees for some minutes, then shyly filed back outside. *What an honor to be the first visitors to the baby King!* they must have thought to themselves. Surely He would have many rich and important visitors soon, and be moved from the cave, but for now joy filled their hearts.

"I can't believe the angels told *us* first!" David commented.

"Maybe the Almighty has a soft spot in His heart for shepherds," Jacob replied.

Shemian shook his head. "I just can't believe it! I just can't believe it."

David chuckled. "I guess the old priest was right."

"I guess he was," Shemian said slowly. "What an honor, for a group of poor shepherds like us! What an honor!"

I nodded. It was an honor, yet I felt stunned and angry that the only people waiting for the Messiah tonight were this tiny group of shepherds on the hillside. The Almighty had given the announcement first to the priests through Zechariah and then all Israel at the Temple. Where was everyone? Certainly not here in Bethlehem.

DAVID

ife, David mused to himself, *just never turns out to be quite what you were expecting. Certainly not my life anyway.* Angrily he kicked at the dust with his bare foot. He had been so excited the night of "the happening," as the shepherds still referred to it. They had seen angels. At least they thought they had—all of them. And they had worshiped the Baby born in the stable, but no one else came. Surely, if this had been the Messiah, someone else would have recognized His existence by now.

The couple with the "Messiah Baby" was as poor as anyone else that that lived in Bethlehem. The young father had done some odd carpentry jobs in the town and earned a little money so that they were able to rent a small one-room house. While it was a little better than a stable, it still seemed far beneath the dignity of a King.

And the baby King was not the only disappointment. Something had happened to his father. He and Mother had been mumbling in low tones, and there had been some crying for several nights. But that often happened between his parents, and he rarely paid attention to it. Before, they had always seemed to work their differences out. But now Father was gone. Mother would not say where, just that he wasn't coming back.

"It makes no sense," Jacob commented to David one day. "If your father wanted to divorce your mother he could have done that. Then he could have still kept the house and his belongings and sent her back to her father. But no, he just disappears. Where did he go?"

"I don't know," David said numbly.

"And your mother will say nothing."

"Well, she hasn't told me anything either, but life without Father is getting harder." Mother had had to sell the flock, so David was no longer a shepherd. Now he hung around town offering to do any odd jobs he could, usually in exchange for food or firewood or other items he and his family needed.

"Well," Jacob sighed, "it's a mystery. But most of these things do come out in the end. Very few things can stay hidden forever, and then everyone will know what evil secret your mother is hiding."

David bristled. "How do you know it's evil?"

"Well, it can't be good. You're living without your father, aren't you?"

Silently David continued to kick the dirt.

"Cheer up," Jacob said. "I heard from my brother that some wealthy foreigners have arrived from Jerusalem. Apparently they came to see King Herod about something that clearly upset him."

"What?" David asked.

"Well, somehow the king has heard of 'the happening here.'"

"Really? Then why didn't he send someone out to honor the little King?"

"I'm not really sure. My brother just said Herod seemed upset. I don't think Herod would like the idea of there being any other kings, Messiah or not. He's always afraid for his throne."

That would be no surprise, David thought to himself. Everyone joked that it was safer to be Herod's pig than his relative in the palace—being a Jew, he wouldn't kill pigs.

"Well," Jacob concluded, "perhaps you will have a chance to meet these foreigners. Maybe you can earn a coin or two watering their camels for them. I've heard they're very generous."

David ran down the dusty path that led out of town toward Jerusalem. Sure enough, Jacob was right. The boy spotted a camel caravan, and it looked like a very wealthy one. Approaching them, David bowed. "May I be of service to you?" he called. "Perhaps I can help you find a place to stay in our fine town, draw water for your beasts?"

Several men seemed to be especially prominent in the caravan and each had a servant or two. The one with the curly beard spoke first. "Yes, boy," he said. "We don't want to stay in any one of those little village inns unless we have to. If there isn't a house we can rent, we'd like to pitch our own camp—if we can do it near your home in a safe place."

"Follow me," David said as he led them toward town. He knew a large open area behind his home on the edge of the village where they could put up their canopies for the night. Everyone knew everyone else in Bethlehem, and now that the registration and taxing was over, it was relatively safe to camp outside.

He stuck his head in the door. "Mother," he shouted, "I brought some people who will be camping outside."

With a sigh she said. "I'll make some more bread." Hospitality could be so demanding.

David watched, amazed as the visitors erected their tents and settled in for the night. Their temporary shelters were nicer than the home he and his family lived in.

"Boy," said the one with the curly beard again, "if you wish to water our camels, we will reward you handsomely. But a word with you first. Have you any important people in this town?"

"Ah, that depends what you mean," the boy answered.

"We are looking for a baby Prince," the man continued. A darker foreigner joined them.

"Yes," he said. "We saw His star in the east. There should be a baby Prince who will grow up to be a great King, and He was born here in this small country. Yet when we went to Jerusalem and inquired of your present king, he knew nothing of this."

"Well, he knows now," chuckled the curly-haired one, "and he wishes us to let him know if we find the Prince so he can come worship Him too."

David raised his eyebrows as did the dark foreigner. "Ah, look at the lad," the man said. "I get the impression he doesn't believe that."

The curly-haired one held out his hand. "A gold coin for your thoughts, boy."

For a moment David stared at the ground. It was dangerous to say things against the Romans, but perhaps a comment about Herod would not get him into too much trouble. The curly-haired one held out the gold coin. David took it.

"I was thinking," he said, "that Herod says many things, but many people who think Herod thinks highly of them end up not thinking at all, because they're dead."

"That is certainly possible," suggested still another of the foreigners who had come to listen. "Courts are always filled with intrigue and treachery."

"Then this one will be no different," David hinted.

"Thank you," the curly-haired one commented, then he gave him another gold coin. "And this is for watering the camels."

David had never had so much money in his life. The coins he had known before had been small and of copper or a shiny white metal. He had seen gold coins held by rich people, but had never actually touched one. "Thank you," he said. "Your camels will be well taken care of."

He led the animals to the trough in the common area of the village and began pulling up bucket after bucket of water. His arms hurt and his back ached, yet those hairy, smelly beasts continued to drink.

"I should have known it would be worth a gold coin to water you," David growled. "I have heard of you evil beasts. You walk for days and days, asking for no water at all, and then you take advantage of a poor boy like me and expect to drink the entire well dry. I think all you camels are a curse."

The camel he spoke to eyed him languidly with its liquid brown eyes and continued to chew its cud, but the one next to it eyed him with cold indifference and then spat.

"Oh, that's disgusting," David complained, wiping the slime from his face and neck. "No more water for you if you're just going to spit." It was a big job, but he finally finished and led the camels back to the campsite.

By now Mother was out talking to the men and had been able to sell them all 12 of the large flat bread loaves she had made.

"Boy," asked the curly-haired one as David tied the last camel to its stake. "Have there been any babies born in this town? We have followed a star from far away, and it led us to Jerusalem and then to this town. Yet you say there is no one rich and important here."

"Well, there is no one rich and important here. However, we did have something odd that some of my friends call 'the happening.'"

The man nodded and drew out another gold coin. "Tell me about it."

"Well, it all started one night when we were out in the field with the sheep. It was lambing time, and so we had to stay out there with them."

David's baby brother began to wail. The boy picked him up, but his mother said, "You go ahead and talk to the men, David. I'll take him in and feed him."

She scooped the child from the little pallet he had been lying on while she passed out the bread to the men and carried him back toward the house while David continued his story.

As David concluded, the men began rapidly speaking to each other in another language. Then the curly-haired one turned back to him. "It is He whom we have come to see. You must take us to Him immediately."

"I can do that," David bowed. "Did you know that my brother was born almost the same time?"

"Oh, that's very nice," the man said, dismissing him with a nod.

"Now take us to the house of the baby Messiah."

David eyed the excited men. "We were wondering if He really was the Messiah since no one has been here from the Temple to worship Him."

The men frowned. "We care nothing for the Temple of the Jews," said the curly-haired one shortly. "We have read the prophecies in ancient scriptures, even Jewish prophecies, and we have seen His star. Why would there be any doubt? Is this not the time even your people expect the Messiah to arrive?"

The lad said nothing.

"Then take us to Him immediately."

Turning, David led the men into the dusty little town to the tiny house rented by the couple. The young mother was playing with her Baby in the shade beside the house. But seeing the men approaching, she scooped Him up and ran inside the dwelling. The men gathered at the doorway, and the curly-haired one spoke again.

"Please don't be afraid," he said. "We have come to worship the Child."

The woman eyed him hesitantly. The father came running from the carpentry project he had been working on two houses over. Again the curly-haired one spoke. "Don't be alarmed. We are not here to hurt your wife or the Child, but to worship Him. My people have seen His star in the east, and we followed it. And we bring gifts."

The father stood with his mouth agape as the servants stepped forward. "We brought you much gold," the curly-haired one explained, "and frankincense and myrrh. Look, these gifts are for Him." Then they fell on their knees. After bowing low, the curly-haired one continued, "I speak for the others, because we are from different places and the languages are difficult. But we all honor the young King. It puzzles us that your country has not honored Him. But they will soon. We told the ruler in Jerusalem about Him."

"Herod?" Joseph asked cautiously.

"Yes," the man nodded. "He said he would like to know where the King was so he could worship Him too."

The couple looked at each other. Mary smiled with delight, but worry and concern flickered across Joseph's face. The Baby started to cry, and the men excused themselves and returned to their campsite.

Young David received more gold and a piece of beautiful eastern silk for his mother. He thanked the men, then returned to his little house. After giving the fabric to his mother, he carefully pried up one of the stones around the fire pit and buried the gold coins there.

His mother nodded. "That is wise, my son. The Lord knows we will need those."

The Almighty did know that, I agreed. That's why He was providing for the events that were just about to burst upon them.

LEVI

THE TEMPLE, JERUSALEM

oung Levi had again accompanied his father to Jerusalem. He loved to spend his days at the Temple watching the people and the sacrifices, learning as much as he could, while his father did his levitical duties. Today, as he often did, the boy sat in the court of women as close to the doorway of the men's court as possible. He liked to see what was going on at the altar of sacrifice. However, many things took place in the court of women too.

Married couples would bring their firstborn child to be blessed at the Temple. All of His people's firstborn had belonged to God ever since the blood on the doorpost had saved the firstborn in Egypt. They had all been His, and every family would pay redemption money in gratitude for the Lord saving their firstborn. Most couples would bring a lamb.

Levi shifted his gaze to a couple approaching the elderly priest. They were carrying two doves, probably bought from one of the dealers in the vast and noisy court of the gentiles. The boy smiled at them. God understood about couples having a hard time making ends meet. That was why He had provided an alternative redemption gift. Poor couples could bring two doves instead.

The couple came to the gateway separating the court of women from the court of Israel. Carefully the father took the sleeping Baby from his wife's arms and ascended the stairs to the court of Israel, where he handed the doves to the officiating priest. Now both Levi and the young mother stood on their tiptoes, straining to see.

With hardly a squawk from them, the priest killed the doves, then climbed up the steps of the great stone altar of sacrifice in the middle of the courtyard and placed their bodies on the fire. Though Levi and the young mother could not see everything happening, they could spot the smoke rising from the altar and hear the singing of the priests and Levites as they offered the special prayers. Now she was no longer unclean. She took a huge breath and let out a sigh of relief. And Levi found himself doing the same thing.

The father returned, and just as he was placing the Baby into the mother's arms, an elderly man named Simeon came huffing across the courtyard. "Wait, wait," he called.

They looked over their shoulders at him. "Us? Does he mean us?"

"I think so," Levi commented. They stood quietly as the old man approached them.

"May I bless the Child?" he asked. The young mother nodded shyly and held the Baby out.

The old man held the Baby up as though He were going to give Him a ritual blessing and then clasped Him to his chest. "Oh, that I have lived to see this day," he sobbed. The young mother shot a worried glance at her husband. "He's the Messiah," whispered the elderly priest. The young mother bowed.

The Messiah? Levi thought. *Is this the baby Zechariah told us about? This would be the right timing. Could it be?*

Simeon continued to bless the Baby and praise the Lord for allowing him to live long enough to see the birth of the Messiah. "Now I can die in peace," he concluded as joyful tears ran down his cheeks.

Just as he was handing the Baby back to his mother, another elderly worshiper hobbled up. "It's Him, isn't it?" she said breathlessly. "He's been born! It's true!"

Mary smiled at her. Levi was so excited he missed most of the conversation. It was true! The Messiah had been born. The timing was perfect according to the prophecies he had heard, as well as according to what Zechariah had told him. And now it had been confirmed by both Simeon and Anna, the Temple grandmother, who, after being widowed in her younger years, had just lived at the Temple, mothering those who needed it.

Levi was so excited that he couldn't sit in the Temple court anymore. Eager to return to where his family was staying, he hopped and skipped and sang praises all the way. Surely the days of the Romans ordering them around were numbered now and everything was going to be all right. The Messiah might be a baby now, but He would grow up quickly.

And I've seen the Messiah, he thought. *Oh, thank You, God!*

DAVID

ut-wrenching screams filled the night and woke David with a start that made his blood run cold. They seemed to be coming from the other side of the village. It was still dark but he spotted lights, perhaps torches, in the direction from which the screams came. His baby brother began to whimper, and Mother held him close to her breast while she said, "Quickly, David, find out what it is. They may need help."

David threw on his outer garment and ran toward the screams. As he rounded the corner, he skidded to a stop and ducked into the shadows. He saw a band of soldiers, perhaps Romans, perhaps Herod's.

"My baby, my baby," one woman shrieked as the men snatched her child from her arms and flung him against the millstone used for grinding flour. David's mouth went dry and he felt his stomach heaving as he stared at the infant lying on the stone, his skull crushed and its sticky contents dripping into the ground next to the stone.

The soldiers went on to the next house. *House to house? Babies?* David thought frantically. *Our baby?*

He sprinted back. "Mother, you've got to hide. They're killing all the babies in town." Quickly she stood and wrapped her cloak around the little one.

"Follow me," David whispered. They slipped out the door and into the back field where the foreigners had camped. Surely they would help hide the little one. He stopped in amazement. There was nothing there. No tents, no camels, just the ashes of the cooking fires.

"But where did they go?" the boy mumbled in surprise. His

mother just stood there, clutching the baby. "Those filthy, good-for-nothing foreigners," David shouted. "They're probably in on this."

"There's another one getting away," a deep voice thundered, and David heard the pounding of running feet.

"Run, Mother," he shouted, but she just stood there as if in a trance.

The soldiers grabbed the infant from her, tearing her cloak as they did so. One of the men tossed the child to the other one. "This one almost got away."

The baby let out a loud wail of protest. The soldier hurled him into the air. A third soldier stuck his spear out and caught the baby on the end of it, impaling him.

David bent over and vomited on the ground, unable to watch anymore. He kept hearing the soldiers laughing, but his mother said nothing. His brother's cries had stopped almost immediately. In a few moments the soldiers moved on.

David stayed curled up on the ground. *There's no point in getting up,* he thought to himself. *There's nothing I can do to save the baby. I have failed. I wasn't able to help Mother; I wasn't able to save the baby.* He just lay there too numb to cry. Finally, as sunlight spilled over the hill and the new day dawned, David could lay there no longer. Wearily he sat up and looked around. Only a bloody patch remained on the grass to indicate what had happened the night before. And that sticky spot was drying. He stood on shaky legs, wiped his face off on the sleeve of his cloak, and staggered back toward the house. Suddenly another thought struck him. *What about the baby Messiah? Surely God wouldn't have allowed the Romans to kill the baby Messiah.*

With a sense of panic he raced toward the house where the couple had lived. It was completely empty. He stood in the doorway, glancing around, confused. But he saw no blood on the floor or walls, and the couple's belongings were gone. They had escaped before the massacre, just like those foreigners who had camped in David's field.

Of course, he thought, *nothing bad would happen to them, just us common people.* He kicked the wall viciously, achieving nothing but a bloody toe. *What an honor to have the Messiah born in our village,* he thought bitterly. *He escapes and is probably just fine somewhere else, having some other rich people bring Him presents while all of our babies have been killed.*

As he shuffled back toward his home he tried not to listen to the weeping families as he passed. Standing in the doorway, he stared into the shadows of their tiny house. His mother sat in the corner, holding a blood-soaked bundle and rocking back and forth, her eyes staring vacantly into space.

"Mother, they're gone," he said. "Everybody's gone."

She didn't answer. "Mother," he asked, "can you hear me?" She continued to rock as if she were in another world. "Mother," he said louder. No response.

I stood recording and watching the groups of guardians in the village clustering together, supporting one another, feeling as sick and grief-stricken as the other inhabitants. It is hard to see not only everything that happens, but also the events leading up to it. Worse yet is to be powerless to do anything to change the course of human choice.

The guardians had warned Joseph and his young wife, and they had fled before the soldiers arrived. The same guardian had appeared in a dream to the Wise Men from the East, warning them not to reveal the birthplace of the baby King to the jealous King Herod. However, Herod had other ways of finding out the Messiah's birthplace. Every male under the age of 2 had been brutally killed in front of his parents and families, who would never be the same again.

Now I had to record the choices of a child who had lost his father and his baby brother and whose mother was locked in a world of her own.

It was almost more than I could bear even as an immortal, and

I gazed with compassion on my grief-stricken human charge. How could the boy survive this?

LEVİ

THE TEMPLE AT PASSOVER, JERUSALEM

he Passover in Jerusalem was a joyful though solemn celebration. Men from all over the country gathered in the holy city, many with their families, to celebrate the festival, for it was one of the mandatory feasts. Also during this time the young men who had completed their twelfth year of life became "the sons of the law," or adults. No longer children, they could now pass from the court of women into the court of Israel and bring their sacrifices. Considered as adults, both legally and spiritually, they were responsible for their own choices. No longer would society hold their parents responsible for what the sons did.

On this occasion I was recording for Levi, and though he was no longer a child (the young ones being my recording specialty), heaven had assigned him to me, for I was familiar with him and fond of the young man. Levi was now 24 and a devout Levite, and though he had been considered legally a man since he was 13, no one was really listened to or treated with complete respect until they had reached at least the age of 30.

Once chomping at the bit to become 13, Levi was now just as eager to be 30 years old. However, human time still ran at the same pace as it did when he was 13—too slow for Levi.

He rested his hand on the shoulder of the young man next to him in a fatherly gesture. "Well, John, now you are a man, and of the priestly line. Your father would be so proud of you." Zechariah's son looked at him, saying nothing.

"I miss him too," Levi continued. "He was like a grandfather to me, and he was very good to my father when he was your age." John nodded but still remained silent.

Frustrated, Levi shook his head. He had tried very hard to help John become a man and learn the things he needed to know, but he was an odd child, very headstrong and quiet. Levi's brow wrinkled. He never knew what John was thinking, and the lad wouldn't reveal his thoughts either. Finally, Levi shrugged. *Someday the boy will speak up and then we'll know what's going on in that head of his, and when that happens, we may not like it.* He smiled to himself. *Perhaps we'll look back on these days and wish he would be silent again.*

He shifted his gaze back to John. "Come on, you son of the law. Now that the priests are through with all of the Passover celebrations, they will gather in the court here. We'll get an opportunity to listen to some of the greatest minds of our day, discussing and debating the law, and any of us that want to can ask questions. It can be fun, and perhaps you'll learn something."

John followed him toward the area where the men were already assembling. Several other new sons of the law had already gathered for their first time to listen to the teachers. They all looked proud and self-conscious and shy at the same time, and were easily distinguished by their young unshaven faces contrasting with the long curly beards of their elders.

Suddenly I felt a jolt of excitement. There He was! I had not received any recording assignments that had brought me close to Him since that horrific night in Bethlehem. Yet here He was, strong and healthy, sitting with the others, a brand new Son of the law, hungry for any pearls of wisdom that might fall from the teachers' lips. What electric joy I felt, for now I could do my job in the presence of the One who had created me.

As I had gazed into His face, last seen on that wobbly little head in Bethlehem so many human years ago, I wondered if He could see me. Or was He limited to human perceptions, having taken on their body. I shook my head. It was beyond my understanding how Someone with infinite capabilities and powers could agree to lower Himself to become a wobbly-necked, helpless little being with all the limitations of this backward race!

I gazed at Him in fascination. He looked just like the other boys. I scanned Him carefully for any traces of divinity, any nuances of the power and glory He had had as my Leader and my King, any hint that He was the Messiah of all the prophecies. Yet I saw nothing except a devout, young adolescent whose eyes burned with devotion and excitement and a hunger for more knowledge, not unlike many others in the group. I continued to watch.

Levi listened with fascination as the priests talked about the coming of the Messiah. One read from Isaiah: "At that time, the Lord will punish the spiritual forces of evil in the heavens above. He will also punish the kings on the earth below. They will be brought together like prisoners in chains. They will be locked up in prison." A ripple of approval surged through the group.

"After many days the Lord will punish them, the Lord who rules over all will rule on Mount Zion and Jerusalem. The elders of the city will be there. They will see His glory. His rule will be so glorious that the sun and the moon will be too ashamed to shine."

"Yes, yes, amen," the men echoed. "Have we had any news of the Messiah coming?" one of them asked.

The priests looked at each other. "No," one replied sadly.

"Perhaps," another countered. They looked at each other for a long time.

"Well, when Zechariah was alive, young John's father, he was told that the Messiah would soon be born."

Several nodded in agreement, as did Levi. "Yes, we remember that," he said. "This means that the Messiah could be among us now as a child or even as a young man here for the Passover."

Everyone nodded, glancing around them, but no one spoke for several minutes. "There were many things said around that time," one priest commented, "a lot of rumors and false starts, and we don't really know what happened. We do know that there were some shepherds who insisted the Messiah had been born in Bethlehem and that they had seen angels, but right after that Herod killed every child there."

One of the young men raised his hand to speak. "Surely our God would not allow the Roman soldiers to kill the Messiah. Surely He would have done something to protect Him."

"Yes, yes," a priest agreed, "and that is why we believe that this was just the imagination of those shepherds."

Levi shot a glance toward an angry-looking young man about his age who stood impassively listening with his arms folded across his chest. "Is that because no angels appeared here at the Temple to the priests?" the stranger asked curtly.

The priests stared at him with a cool and level gaze. "Yes," he said. "The Scriptures say plainly that God does not do anything but that He reveals it to His servants the prophets."

"Hum," the young man responded. "But He did reveal it to the prophets—several of them, as we're so fond of quoting. 'But thou, Bethlehem, though thou be least . . .' "

"Yes, yes, yes," the priest replied. "We have no argument with the place, only the timing and the unreliable sources. By the way, what is your name, young man?"

"David."

"Ah," said the priest, "and I suppose you've talked to one of those insane shepherds who was out there at the time?"

"In a manner of speaking," David answered curtly.

"Well, then you know that they cannot have been well-schooled in the law. They were just eager for the Messiah to come as we all are, and thus you can't blame them for getting a little overexcited."

Turning on his heel, David walked away.

I watched sadly. So much pain and loss in such a short life. No wonder he was bitter. I turned back to Levi, my assignment for today.

"Getting back to what you said," he addressed the rabbi, "if He was among us now, it would only be a few years before He would be a man and start His ministry and throw the Romans out. We might have only a few years to wait."

Another young man raised his hand and asked to talk. "Isaiah does speak of wonderful times when the world will be ruled from Jerusalem and everyone will love the Almighty and worship Him, but is that speaking of the Messiah when He comes, or about the end of times? In many places Isaiah says specifically that he is speaking of the end of times.

"What about the verses that declare that the Lord's Servant, when He comes, will be a suffering servant," the youth continued. "Or what about the verses where it tells how people looked down on Him, refusing to accept Him? How He knew all about sorrow and suffering? And how He was like someone that people turn their faces away from?

"What about where it says 'He was pierced because we had sinned; He was crushed because we had done what was evil. He was punished to make us whole again, and His wounds have healed us. All of us, like sheep, have wandered away from God and turned to our own way, and the Lord has placed on His Servant the sins of us all'?"

"Yes," one of the priests said slowly, "sometimes it can be confusing to those who are not schooled in the Scriptures, for there are many passages that speak this way about the Messiah."

I was impressed with the way the young Yeshua respectfully asked His questions and kept drawing the teachers and priests back to the prophecies of the suffering servant and to the sacrificial lamb analogies. Since it tied in so well with the sacrificial system, many in the group started agreeing with Him. "Yes, we've been sacrificing sheep all these years, looking forward to the Messiah. Could the Messiah be a sacrifice?"

While a few agreed, others protested that what they really needed was a military Messiah who would overthrow the Romans and save the country.

"The Messiah would know," one of them argued, "that first things are first. He would need to liberate this country and give us our physical freedom before He started addressing spiritual issues. After all, there is a hierarchy of need, you know."

"But," the young Yeshua persisted, "being the God of Israel, would He not be most concerned with saving His people from their spiritual distress, rather than their physical conditions? Would not our spiritual issues really be the most important?"

The discussion went on and I watched in fascination. Even as a youth, Yeshua was drawing everyone's attention to the Scriptures and making them think. Gently, with His questions, He was leading them to conclusions without forcing anything down their throats in the domineering manner of so many teachers.

Yes, He was the true Messiah. And it would only be a short time before many of these humans would recognize it.

On the third day of the rabbinical discussions, young Yeshua was still amazing everyone with His questions. Then about midday an anxious man entered the room and started scanning the crowd.

"Yeshua," he said, trying not to be too disruptive. "Yeshua."

The Youth looked up and obediently rose and went to His father. "Yeshua, we've been looking everywhere for You. Your mother is waiting in the outer court. Please come with us now."

The others turned and watched and chuckled as the young Man followed obediently. On impulse Levi followed Him. When He entered the court of women, Yeshua's mother flung her arms around Him. "Son, why did You do this to us? We've been so worried about You. We looked everywhere," she said, bursting into tears.

He hugged her and stroked her hair gently. "Why were you looking for Me, Mother?" He asked. "Didn't you know it's now time for Me to be doing My Father's business? Didn't you know you'd find Me right here in His house?"

She pulled back and looked deep into His eyes, then nodded her head slowly. Gently He wiped the tears away. "Come," He said, "let's go home."

The older man walked silently as the woman and her Son seemed to share some special bond. Levi's brow furrowed deep in thought. Somehow he felt that he had seen this woman somewhere before, but where? When?

I smiled. *You'll know soon, Levi,* I thought to myself. This is all fitting together so well.

SAMUEL

JORDAN RIVER

amuel walked briskly next to his father as they headed down the last embankment of the rocky Judean hillside toward the Jordan River. The sparkling water and lush greenery looked inviting after the dusty wilderness of steep crags and deep ravines they had crossed the past two days.

"Look, Father, there's already a bunch of people down there."

His father stared. "Yes, though it's early in the day, apparently we are not the first to come hear the preacher."

"Do you think he could be the Messiah?"

"I don't know," his father said after a pause. "That's why I wanted to listen to him for myself."

"Some people say that he is," the boy continued. "Wouldn't it be wonderful if he was? We've waited so long."

"Yes," the father said. "It would be wonderful, and we are close to the time. There have been many prophecies and strange events. Mathias tells me that this John has lived in the desert ever since his father died and that he wears camel hair."

"Isn't that what the prophet Elijah always wore? In the stories that's what we were told."

"Yes, and not only does he dress like Elijah, but he has all of his boldness too. When you hear some of the things that the Baptist is supposed to have said, you realize that it takes every bit as much nerve to say those things to people in power as it did for Elijah to challenge King Ahab and Queen Jezebel."

Samuel thought a moment. "I have heard that some people be-lieve he is the prophet Elijah brought back to life to let us know that the Messiah is coming, while other people think he is the Messiah Himself."

"Well," Father replied, "we could just ask him outright. Surely if we did, he would have to tell us the truth."

"Would that place him in danger—for us to ask something like that? You can see soldiers mingled in with the common people."

"Well, soldiers aren't his only worry. There are always the spies from the scribes and the Pharisees. With the high priest's job going to the highest bidder and controlled by the Romans, they would hardly have a use for a Messiah right now. It could ruin all their plans."

"Well, he doesn't seem to be the cautious type, though, according to what we've heard," Samuel commented.

"No, but then what use have we for a cautious Messiah?" They both laughed. "Stay close," Father said. "This crowd is huge. I wouldn't want to have to go looking for you in there."

The boy studied the crowd. "If we get separated, let's meet toward the end of the day over by that canyon." He pointed to one farther down river from the crowd.

"Good idea," his father agreed. "Still I'd rather you stay close."

Although the crowd was large, the Baptist had a strong voice, and it echoed off the cliffs so that everyone could hear him. "The time has come," he shouted. "The Messiah is going to be here soon. It is no longer something that we are prophesying for your children's children. Are you ready? Can you stand in front of Him with a clear conscience?"

A murmur broke through the crowd. A man stepped forward. "Who is it?" asked those who could not see clearly.

"It's Matthew, the tax collector." Someone spat on the ground. "Sniveling little collaborator. What does he want with the preacher?"

Matthew bowed his head. "What can I do?" he asked the preacher. "You know I am a tax collector, as are my friends here. What can we do to be prepared to stand before the Messiah?"

John looked at the man gently, realizing that everyone hated his type, both those they collected taxes for and those they collected taxes from. "You need to collect no more than what is appointed for you," he replied. "Stop cheating the people."

Matthew let out a sigh of relief. A civilized country, even an occupied one such as theirs, needed tax collectors, and according to John's statement, being one would not keep him from being acceptable to the Messiah. Samuel watched as the Baptist preached, then paused to answer questions from those in the crowd. Those who came forward he would lead out into the water and baptize.

"What is he doing?" asked Samuel.

"I don't know," said his father. "It looks as if they confess their sins and he instructs them how to live. John then buries them in the water. What he is doing is like regular immersion in the mikvah [ritual bathing place], but more than that. Perhaps it symbolizes all of their old ways being washed away so that they can start new and fresh."

Samuel stared at his father thoughtfully. "That sounds really good."

His father sighed. "I don't know about you, son, but there are things I would be happy to bury in the Jordan and not carry guilt for anymore."

His son stood in thought for a moment. "Let's do it!" he suddenly said. The father looked at him and smiled. They both struggled through the crowd. As Samuel and his father pressed toward the water's edge, the two men in front of them reached the Baptist first.

"Baptize us too, rabbi," they said. "We want to be ready to meet the Messiah."

The Baptist turned and looked at them. The buzzing crowd fell silent as he continued to stare at them. Then with fiery eyes John shouted, "You slithering bunch of snakes. You think that you'll strengthen your influence with the people because you've been baptized here, but you care nothing about repentance. Hasn't anyone warned you about the wrath to come? You keep insisting that you're children of Abraham, but that means nothing to God. He judges every tree by its fruit, and if the fruit is worthless, the tree will be destroyed no matter what its name is."

The men retreated before every new accusation the Baptist made. Soon they backed right into Samuel and his father. As the Baptist continued to expose their true character, the men melted into the crowd and vanished.

Samuel shook his head. "They're really going to hate him now."

Reluctantly his father nodded. The boy almost felt afraid to step forward now. It seemed that the Baptist had the ability to read minds, or else God was whispering in his ear exactly what each person was. But taking a deep breath, Samuel approached the preacher anyway. "I would like to be baptized," he said, his voice cracking as he spoke.

. The Baptist lowered his gaze to Samuel. "Come closer, my son," the austere man said. "In your daily life be fair and merciful, and the love of God will be seen in you. God's followers should be kind and honest and truthful. Care about the poor and the needy and remember to bring your offerings to God. And always defend those who can't stick up for themselves."

Samuel nodded. As the boy rose from the water of the Jordan River, he felt as if he tingled with new life. He was not only a son of Abraham, he was totally committed to being a child of God, and when the Messiah was revealed, he would be His follower too. Filled with great joy, he almost didn't notice that John baptized his father right behind him.

The two of them stood dripping on the bank, watching as the Baptist continued to preach. "Are you cold, son? Do you want to leave and get some dry clothes?"

Samuel shook his head. "I'd like to listen a little while longer. I'm not cold. In fact, I feel wonderful."

His father laughed. "So do I, son; so do I."

Three Roman soldiers now pushed their way to the front of the crowd. "We wish to be baptized too," they said.

A murmur rippled through the crowds. "Romans? Foreigners? The Messiah is for our people. Surely His very coming would be a threat to such men. Why would they want to be baptized?" But the preacher was unflappable. He turned his deep stare on them.

To the first one he said, "You must stop intimidating people. You abuse your power and push them around, especially the weak or those unable or afraid to push back."

All three soldiers seemed to catch their breath. The second one nudged the first, saying, "He's right, Longenius."

"I repent," Longenius said humbly, "and I wish to be baptized."

The Baptist nodded. "Then you shall be."

The second one stepped forward. "My name is Brutus, and I too wish to be baptized."

John the Baptist studied him closely. "You must not falsely accuse people," he said, "and you must not make money from your false accusations, but be honest and upright." The soldier's jaw dropped; it was as if the preacher had stared into his very soul and exposed his secrets to the crowd.

The third soldier stepped forward and bowed his head. "And you," John continued, "must be content with your wages. Do not use your authority in hurtful ways to increase your power or increase your income by cheating or stealing. And do not complain about receiving a fair wage."

The third soldier nodded silently. Then to the shock and horror of the crowd, John baptized the three Romans.

Samuel turned to his father. "He never told them to stop serving Rome or to quit being soldiers. Why? Does this mean they can be baptized and be acceptable to the Messiah without quitting their jobs as soldiers? Surely that would be a minimum requirement. Surely they would join the bands of zealots fighting for the freedom of our country. Isn't the Messiah going to overthrow the Romans?"

"I don't know anymore, Samuel. I'm confused. This is what I believe, yet the Baptist did not tell us to do anything of a violent nature. I think we need to return home and do exactly what he told us. And my bet is Longenius and Brutus and whoever else was with them will do the same. Perhaps the Messiah will give us other instructions later, but until then this is all we can do."

The crowd was still discussing the soldiers as a nondescript Man stepped forward. Yeshua smiled. "I wish to be baptized," He said.

"No, no, I can't do that," John, His cousin, protested. "You should be baptizing me. How can I do this? You have nothing for which to repent."

Yeshua smiled again. "It is true. I do not seek baptism as a confession of guilt, but as an opening of My ministry. I am ready to do the will of God. My baptism will be the unsheathing of My sword, ready to do battle."

John bowed his head as if in submission. "Come," he said. "I will."

Wading into the water, John buried Yeshua under the sparkling ripples. Samuel watched in fascination. The Man's lips moved as if He were praying, but Samuel couldn't hear the words because of the distance and the noise of the crowd.

I listened carefully, for the Son of the Most High was praying for His Father's blessing at the start of His ministry. He was definitely identifying with His human brothers and sisters and was feeling the horror and the depth of the sin around Him. The Son of the Almighty could tell how it had hardened the hearts of the people there and how difficult it would be for them to understand His mission, much less accept His gift of salvation from the Father. As He prayed, He pleaded with the Father for the power both to overcome their unbelief and to break the chains of sin that bound them. Most of all, He begged His Father to accept Him. The Son of the Almighty longed for affirmation. In amazement I realized that His humanity was such that even He needed encouragement and affirmation. Instantly I signaled the Command Center. I would be happy to rush to His side and give Him the assurance He asked for. I am certain that every other immortal present that day was busy signaling too, probably jamming the Control Center. However, we all got a negative reply as the Father Himself affirmed His Son. As we looked heavenward, the clouds parted, and a shaft of light shone down on the quiet, dripping Galilean still standing in the water.

Samuel noticed a white dove float silently down and land on Yeshua's shoulder.

"Look, Father," the youth said, poking his father. "Look!" His father shrugged. "That dove doesn't seem to be afraid of anything, does it?

Then the Father's voice declared, "This is My precious Son, and I am pleased with Him. Listen to Him."

Samuel turned in delight. "Father, did you hear that?"

"Yes," his father replied, "it sounded like thunder. It's too early for the rainy season to begin."

"No," the boy protested, "I heard a voice." By this time the break in the clouds had closed. The light was gone, and Yeshua made His way up the embankment as others pressed forward to request baptism.

John turned and pointed at the receding figure. "Look," he declared. "It is the Lamb of God. He is going to take away the sins of the world." The crowd turned, but saw no one who appeared unusual.

"Perhaps He's prophesying," Father commented.

"No," Samuel insisted, "it's that Person over there."

"Probably not," his father sighed. "Prophets are always a little odd. Sometimes they're difficult to understand."

"You didn't hear it?" his son asked.

His father studied him slowly. "I think it's time we went and got dry clothes on," he said finally.

Samuel fell silent, and the two headed back toward the nearest village. Although the boy tried to make sense of what he had seen that afternoon, it was no use. With a shrug he followed his father up the muddy path.

"Rabbi," a man from the crowd behind them shouted at John, "are you the Messiah for whom we've been waiting?"

John turned toward the voice. "No; I am but a messenger."

"Then you are Elijah," the man yelled back. "It was prophesied that you would come before the Messiah to help us prepare for Him."

The Baptist nodded. "I am here to help prepare His way. He is coming, and soon. The One coming is so much greater than I. I am not even good enough to help Him take off His dirty sandals at the end of the day and wash His feet."

The murmuring kept rippling through the crowd. "Truly he is speaking about the Messiah. And it sounds as if He should appear any day now. How wonderful! No more Romans, no more sin, no more unbelievers. Everyone will worship God, and Jerusalem will be the capital of the world! I can't wait. Praise the Almighty to think we've lived to see this day!"

MARK

JUDEAN DESERT

hile I was neither assigned to be His recorder or His guardian, I was allowed to follow and observe as the Son of the Almighty left the river and headed toward the Judean wilderness. Many during this time period believed the desert to be a place where spirits constantly battled, and certainly this time it would be just such a place.

My fellow immortals and I watched with amazement as our Creator and our King, the Son of the Most High, suffered extreme heat, hunger, and thirst as He spent all His time in prayer and preparation for the task ahead of Him. We longed to relieve His suffering, checking continually with the Command Center to see if we were allowed to bring Him food and encouragement, but we were not. To our horror He struggled with doubts and difficulties both mental and physical.

For 40 days of human time we waited. Finally His preparation was complete. He was ready to start His ministry, but His body was on the verge of collapse.

Suddenly our archenemy chose to reveal his presence. So far he had worked all the temptation and suffering through his messengers. Now he planned to finish the job himself. He appeared as bright and glorious as any of us as he unveiled himself to Yeshua. The once Creator King, now a starving and emaciated human being, stared at the glorious angel. The tempter held bread. Its aroma wafted over to Yeshua, almost bringing tears to His eyes. "Yes," Lucifer said, "it's every bit as delicious as it smells. Would you like some?"

Yeshua just continued to gaze at him silently. "I heard what happened down at the river," the tempter continued. "Very impressive, so if that's really true and You really are the Son of God—which seems rather unlikely judging by Your present physical state—why don't You just turn these stones littering the ground into bread? Surely You'll be unable to do whatever mission the Almighty has in mind if You starve to death and don't make it out of the desert here. It would pretty much put an end to that plan, wouldn't it?" Then he laughed.

"Eating is not the most important thing in the world," Yeshua replied quietly. "My Father is quite able to take care of Me and execute His plan without Me abusing My power selfishly."

We all were aware that the enemy is unable to read human minds, although at times he claims that ability. Indeed, he has watched humans since he tricked them into joining his rebellion and has a good idea of their personality and character. From their facial expressions he can guess pretty well what they are thinking. In addition, he can project thoughts and pictures and images into the human mind, and this is what we observed him doing next.

With Yeshua, Son of the Almighty, already in a weakened condition, it was not difficult to make it seem to Him that He and the rebel were standing on the pinnacle of the Temple just above the steep wall that fell away to the Kidron Valley.

It was such a height that a fall would be fatal. "If You're really the Son of God, as You would have us believe," the enemy said, "why don't You just jump? If You are the promised Messiah, God will have to rescue You. That will be good for You and good for Your ministry, because then everyone will see and know that You are the Messiah. You won't have to spend years trying to convince them. They will believe You and just follow You, completing God's plan much sooner."

Yeshua's forehead wrinkled into a frown. "It is written in the Scriptures," He answered, "that we should not tempt the Lord our God. Jumping from here would be foolish, and trying to force Him into a situation to prove something is hardly submitting to His will."

After a brief silence the enemy took Yeshua to a high mountain and showed Him the whole world. Then he said in a friendly tone, "You know, Yeshua, I really am on Your side. I understand how hard it is to be sent to this particular planet. It's a depressing place, and I've been here longer than You. But I understand how things work here, and I am on Your side. If You will just bow and swear allegiance to me, I'll take care of things for You."

"Take care of things for Me?" Yeshua echoed.

"Sure. I can give You all the power You need. I have control over everyone in the high places—in government and in the Judean resistance. Together we could take care of things, and I could make You the ruler of this planet with very little difficulty. Your life would be much easier. A lot easier than the plan You seem to be following right now."

All of us watching were furious at what the enemy implied, in addition to being angry that he would pick a time when the Son of our King was at His most vulnerable. Yet we needn't have worried. Yeshua had no intention of bowing to the rebel. "The Scriptures say that we should worship the Lord only, and He is the only One I will bow to."

Shaking with rage and humiliation, the enemy vanished. For a second we gave cheers of victory, then suddenly lapsed into silence as the Son of God fell to the ground. Pale and blue about His lips, He appeared to be dying. All of us again flashed messages to the Command Center. "Can we help Him? We're right here. We're ready."

I received an affirmative. Me? A lowly recording angel? Although not one of the warriors or the guardians, I still received this tremendous honor. Immediately I materialized and rushed to His side to comfort Him with the affirmation of His Father's love, the assurance that all of us were triumphing in His victory. Heaven allowed several others also to gather about Him, giving Him food and water and nursing Him back from the edge of death.

Never will humans fully understand what He went through, enduring every test that they will ever encounter, every temptation or trial that they might ever imagine and more—and He emerged the victor. No human will ever be able to say that He can't understand what they endure, because He *can*. And every human will be able to gain their own victory through submission and faith in God, even as Yeshua, Son of the Almighty, did. They can just use the name of the Lord. The enemy will tremble and flee before even the weakest soul who calls out that mighty name for help. How comforting it must be for them to know this, and what an honor it was for my companions and me as we fed Him and cared for Him that hot afternoon in the Judean wilderness. It is a day I will never forget.

RACHEL

CANA

ary, how wonderful to see you," Rachel cried as she flung her arms around her friend. "It's been so long."

Her friend's eyes filled with tears.

"Oh, I'm sorry, Mary. I know that the past few years have been painful for you. It must be hard without Joseph."

The tears spilled down Mary's cheeks. "It is, but Yeshua has been such a comfort to me. We've always been close. Although it is an embarrassment to the family that He's not married yet—but then He's never wanted to do things the way the rabbi suggested."

"Is he coming to the wedding?" Rachel asked.

"I certainly hope so. He's been gone for two months now. I miss Him greatly."

"I'll bet you do. I heard he went to the Baptist at the Jordan."

Rachel's friend nodded.

"And that He went off somewhere in the wilderness and no one has seen Him since."

Mary's pain was almost palpable. "Well, He knows this wedding is coming up, and He knows when it is, and I am hoping that He will show up for it. Even though the bride is much younger than the rest of them, He loves all of His cousins and holds a special spot in His heart for her. I'm sure He'll be here if He can—and if He's all right."

I knew that Mary couldn't help worrying. Even though she had been told who her Son was, she also had periods of doubt and concern. She longed for the time when He would reveal His glory, declare Himself the Messiah, and take over the government of the now broken and occupied country. He had been just a dutiful and obedient Son, living at home and helping her through the difficult adjustment to widowhood until two months ago. Then He had put down His tools, hugged her tenderly, and told her it was time for Him to leave. His siblings were relieved that He was at least doing something. After all, a man of His age should have been married and producing offspring by now. Yet He had been content to work in His father's shop and care for His parents.

Mary sighed and thought, *Joseph. If Yeshua really was the Messiah, couldn't He have done something to help His father? He had been a good husband and loving father to Him.*

Then wiping her face, she forced a smile. "So what can I help you with, Rachel? There must be many things still to be done."

Rachel laughed. "Come, let me show you what I have been cooking." At that moment she glanced down the road and, covering her mouth with her hand, squealed, "He's here; He's coming up the hill right now and He's got several friends with Him."

"My Son?" Mary asked, her face shining with joy. Rushing toward Him, she hugged Him tighter than she ever had before. "Oh, Yeshua, I'm so glad to have You here! I'm so glad You came to the wedding. Oh, You look—" She paused and studied Him. He didn't seem the same. His face appeared as if He had been through some great ordeal, and yet He'd been gone only two months.

Yes, something most unusual had happened, and He had obviously experienced great pain. Yet He wrapped her in a huge bear hug and swung her feet clear off the ground. "I'm glad to see you, too, Mother," He said, then set her down. "I'm sure you've been busier than a bee helping Aunt Rachel with everything here."

"Oh, yes, it's going to be a wonderful feast. We have so much food. Everything is just perfect!"

"Good," He commented, chuckling, "because you and Aunt Rachel would never rest until it was."

His mother laughed. He was always teasing her about her need for perfection in a kind way that seemed to reassure her that, whether or not things really were perfect, He would love her just as much. Taking her hand in His massive calloused one, He introduced her to His friends.

They all showed great deference to Him, as if He was an honored rabbi. *Well, after all,* she thought, *He is their promised Messiah.*

Afterward the little group proceeded into the courtyard of Rachel's home to prepare for the party.

A couple days later I stood by watching as Rachel sobbed into her towel just outside the kitchen courtyard area. "What a humiliation," she wailed. "What will all the guests think? All the food is perfect, and we have so much, yet we've run out of wine. What are they going to drink?"

She heard footsteps behind her and quickly dried her face. "Rachel, what's the matter?" her old friend inquired.

"Oh, Mary, you'll never believe this. There's nothing left to give them to drink. We were so concerned about the house being clean and perfect and having enough food, it never occurred to me they would drink up all the wine in the first few days."

Mary's mouth dropped open. It would be a dreadful social blunder not to have enough wine. Instinctively she reached for her money pouch hanging at her waist; then her hand dropped to her side again. She and Joseph had never been wealthy, but since her widowhood times had been even tighter. If she'd had any money to purchase wine, she would have given every coin to her best friend.

Wrapping her arms around Rachel, she said on impulse, "I will go talk to my Son about it."

"What can He do? He hasn't worked for two months and will have no more money than you do."

Mary drew herself up to her full height in dignified protest. "I didn't mean to hurt your feelings," Rachel gasped. "It's just that I don't know what to do."

"I'll be back," Yeshua's mother told her quietly.

I watched Rachel collapse into another paroxysm of weeping. Several minutes later the servants came through the kitchen area toward the water jars where she was sobbing. Quickly she dried her face and walked away, hoping they had not noticed.

What are they doing with the water jars? she thought. *Just when we're having a crisis, they want to fill the water jars?* She shook her head in disgust. Servants!

Crossing the courtyard, she headed back toward the feast. "This may be the ultimate disgrace," she said to herself, "but I can carry myself with dignity." From where she sat with the other women, she could see that her husband and the other men were having their cups refilled. Rachel glanced at Mary. "They must have found a little more," she said to her. Mary just smiled in response.

"What wonderful wine!" one of the men boomed. "You sly fox," he said to her husband. "Most people would serve the best wine first and save their cheaper vintage for last, yet you've saved the very best until the third day. It is delicious!"

Rachel's husband just beamed at his wife, who smiled back, pretending to understand what was going on. Then the servants brought wine to the women's table, and Rachel tasted it. "Is there any more?" she whispered to the servant who had filled her cup.

"Yes, my lady," he replied. "Three times as much as we had to start with."

"Where did it come from?"

"Your friend," he nodded toward Mary, "said that whatever her Son told us to do, we should do it. We thought He was crazy. He ordered us to refill the water jars."

"Yes," Rachel nodded. "I saw you doing that."

"Well, then He directed us to dip some water from it and take it to the head of the men's table. That's what the roar was about. When we poured the water from the serving jug, it was this!" She took another sip.

"It tastes wonderful," she exclaimed.

"Yes," the servant agreed. "I had a little taste myself to make sure it was OK."

Rachel turned to Mary and beamed. Her friend smiled back. "It's a miracle!" Rachel whispered.

"He said it wasn't His time," Mary replied. "He's always been such an obedient Son to me, but now He said He had another job to do. But it must be God rewarding Him for His obedience or me for my faith in Him. Or perhaps He loves you, or He just approves of this wedding. But yes, we have a miracle!"

And I smiled, for all of those things were true and so much more—more than they could ever understand.

Andrew

VILLAGE OF MAIN

awn was just streaking the sky when Andrew returned to the house carrying the large jug of water. Hauling water was women's work, but since his father had died, his mother had seemed so fragile that Andrew just made it a point to go to the well early in the morning before she had a chance to. And she gratefully allowed it.

This morning as he approached the house he saw her already baking the flat loaves of bread in the rounded mud-brick oven in the courtyard. "You're up early," he said. "Already you've got the bread baking."

"I'm excited," she said with a smile.

"Oh." It had been a long time since he'd seen a sparkle in his mother's eye. "What's happening?"

"Yeshua from Nazareth is coming through here today. I've heard so many wonderful things about Him."

Her son nodded. He too was curious to meet this former carpenter and now itinerant teacher.

"I'm going to take you to Him," she said. "I want Him to bless you. He is no ordinary young rabbi. Many people are whispering that He is the Messiah. Someday He will be really famous, and you will be able to say that He blessed you when you were young. Perhaps when He throws out the Romans and sets up His government in Jerusalem, He may have a position for you. You never know. It's always good to have connections. And even if nothing else, at least you can tell your children and grandchildren that you heard Him speak."

"Well, then, let me feed the animals quickly so that we'll be ready."

While Andrew took care of the animals I watched his mother pack a lunch—cheese curds, some dried fruit, and the freshly baked flat bread. Their chores done, the mother and son headed for the edge of town. Two hills fairly close together provided a perfect natural amphitheater. They wanted to find a good place to sit where they could hear and hopefully approach the Teacher and ask His blessing.

When they arrived, what they saw disheartened them. "Look, Mother, hundreds of people have gotten here ahead of us. Now we'll never get to talk to the Teacher."

"Yes, we will," she replied with a determined jut to her jaw.

Andrew grinned. When his mother got that look on her face she always figured out a way to do what she wanted no matter who opposed her.

Andrew held her elbow protectively as they pressed through the crowd. He didn't want her to get lost. The Teacher sat on a large rock at the center. Only a few more feet and they could talk to Him. The knot of men who always seemed to be around Him now was the only thing between the young Teacher and Andrew's determined mother.

"Rabbi," she called. "Rabbi, please bless my son."

Yeshua turned to see where the request was coming from. But his disciples blocked His view.

"Stop it," hissed one of the bearded men at Mother. "Can't you see He has more important things to do? Be silent, woman, and sit down. Women these days just don't know their place. And you too." He turned to Andrew. "What is your name, boy?"

"Andrew."

"Well, Andrew, get your mother out of here and sit down."

Another disciple smiled at the boy. "Don't let his gruffness scare you," he said. "His name is Andrew too."

While the two Andrews stared at each other, Mother called out again, "Rabbi, Yeshua of Nazareth, please bless my son."

The disciple named Andrew frowned. "Woman, I told you . . ."

But a voice behind him stopped him cold.

"Andrew," Yeshua said, "let the children come to me. Don't chase them away. The kingdom of heaven is going to be made of boys just like this."

"I told you," Mother said. "He's going to have a spot for you in His kingdom." The adult Andrew frowned.

I smiled as the younger Andrew wiggled his way through the men to Yeshua's side. The Son of the Almighty looked into the boy's eyes, then placed His hand on his shoulder and blessed him. "I do have a spot for you in my kingdom," he said, "though it may not be exactly what you imagine."

Andrew wanted just to sit at His feet and listen all day, but other children and their mothers crowded around. The boy found his mother and helped her over to a good spot on the hillside for hearing and seeing everything that happened.

* * *

"Andrew," his mother began one day a few weeks later, "I hear that Yeshua of Nazareth is going to be near my old childhood home this week."

"Really? That's a long way from here. We could walk, but we would not be able to get there and back the same day."

"No, we wouldn't, but perhaps we could stay in my uncle's home overnight. If we leave tomorrow we can arrive there for the night and then hear the Preacher the next day. Perhaps we can even stay that night and head home the next morning. After all, we have not imposed on my uncle's hospitality for many years."

A tinge of bitterness crept into her voice. Andrew was oblivious to it, but I was not. I had been recording in her uncle's village for another child when the boy's mother was young, and I remembered how he resented having to care for his nieces when his brother died. He did not treat them well and married them off as quickly as he was able to so that someone else would have to support them. She must really want to see Yeshua again to be willing to go there.

Andrew, knowing none of this, was delighted. "An overnight trip!" he shouted. "That's wonderful! I will talk to Amos and see if he will take care of our lambs and chickens while we are gone. You know he will do anything for those little cakes you make. He loves your cooking. His family may have more money than us, but his mother doesn't cook as well as you do."

Mother laughed. "Not all women are the same," she said. "We all have talents, but they're different. I'm glad that Amos likes my cakes."

Her son smiled. "I'll go talk to him right away so that we can get ready to go."

She nodded as she gathered some provisions for the journey. Though she would request shelter and a safe place to sleep, she planned to take her own food and ask nothing else from her uncle even though society expected him to provide all those things.

The trip was long, hot, and dusty, but Andrew enjoyed the time spent with his mother. As they chatted away she told him stories about his father.

"How did you and Father meet?" he asked.

"We met at our wedding," said Mama. "I was very young, and though I was too young to be married, my uncle had us betrothed very early on and convinced your father's family that if I came to their home, I would be a better wife having grown up with their son. So we were married very young, and I came to live with him."

"Weren't you afraid?"

"A little bit. I did not know whether your father was going to be a kind person or a cruel one. He was much older than me, but ever since my parents had died, and I had been living with my uncle, I had been very unhappy. I figured it couldn't be any worse than that."

"So what happened next?"

"I came to live in your father's home. And though he was much older than me, he was very kind. All of his family was kind. And he treated me like the little girl that I was until I was older. Your father was a blessing from God—and I miss him," she said, her voice cracking a little.

The boy reached over and squeezed her arm. "I know you do, Mother. I do too. But I'm glad God gave you a good man."

She nodded. "It is a much greater blessing to have a good man for a short time than a cruel one for a long time. God has been good to me, and now my greatest blessing is you!

"Just think," she said to him. "Without you, I would have no value at all. Because of you, I was able to stay in the home that your father left us and to keep the sheep and the chickens and continue life in Nain as we have. If I had not had you, Andrew, I would have had to return to my uncle."

"If that had happened he would have taken you back, wouldn't he?" Andrew inquired.

"I don't know. But thankfully, the Lord sent you, and you're able to inherit your father's property. God is good."

"God is good," her son echoed.

They came over the brow of the hill, and Mother caught her breath. "There it is. There's my home where I lived as a little child."

Andrew frowned. "Why was your uncle so eager to get rid of you? It looks as if they are well off. He has many more animals than we do, and a vineyard."

"Yes, he has lots of land. He also owns a few of those little houses over there that he rents to other farmers."

"Then he could afford to take care of you," her son protested.

"Affording was not the problem, but let's not talk of those days. Those days were days of tears for me, but now the Lord has been so good to me, and even though I have lost my husband, I still have you, so let's not think about that. Let's be happy to see Uncle, and perhaps he'll even be happy to see us."

The rest of the way did not seem long at all, and soon they were at the doorstep. A servant ushered them in. They were just having a drink of water when Mother's uncle burst into the room.

"What are you doing here?" he demanded. "Have you squandered your husband's money and now want to sponge off me?"

"No, we ask nothing except your hospitality," she replied. "We would like to stay tonight here in your home."

"Why? Where are you going?"

"Yeshua of Nazareth is preaching near here."

"Yes, I know," the uncle snapped. "That Man is a nuisance. The servants are always wanting to sneak off and talk to Him, and no one wants to get any work done around here."

"Well," she continued, "we have traveled here and wish to go hear Him speak tomorrow. If you will let us sleep in your home in safety, that's all we ask."

"Well, don't expect the servants to wait on you hand and foot."

"We even brought our own provisions. I expect nothing from you. I know better than that."

Her uncle raised his hand and slapped her. "You worthless female; don't you insult me."

Andrew drew himself to his full height and stepped in between his great-uncle and his mother. Saying nothing, he just stood there, staring his great-uncle in the face. The man glared, raised his hand again, and then backed away. Perhaps he could sense the guardians clustering around Andrew.

"All I can say is you're lucky to have that boy. You were worthless as a child and you would be worthless as a widow if you didn't have that son. All I can say is you're lucky."

Turning, he stomped away. After he disappeared, Mother burst into tears. Andrew tried to comfort her.

"It's true what he said," she said. "I have no value without you now that your father is gone."

"But you do have me," Andrew replied. "I'll never leave you, Mother, never. Don't worry about the future."

Andrew and his mother awoke before dawn and slipped out of the house. It was easier to leave before Uncle was up. They sat on the hillside and listened to Yeshua of Nazareth speak. Andrew was delighted. It was as if the Teacher had been hiding in the corner listening to their conversation the night before. Everything He said encouraged Andrew and his mother. When Yeshua said, "Blessed are you that mourn, for you will be comforted," it especially caught the boy's attention.

He hugged his mother. The Teacher had not only blessed Andrew but his mother, too. She was just as important. Sure enough, later in His sermon He talked about what great value God placed on everyone. It was as if He had heard the uncle's cruel words the night before when He declared: "God sees even the little sparrow fall, and you have more value than many sparrows." The light came back into Mother's eyes. No matter how hard things were, it seemed that Yeshua of Nazareth knew exactly what the pain in her heart was, and He understood.

"Mother," Andrew announced a few days later, "the Teacher is going to be not too far from here tomorrow. I've heard He's coming this way. Can we listen to Him again?"

She straightened up, her hand rubbing the small of her back. "Andrew, you may go with Jonathan if you like," she said. "I will not be able to go this time. Miriam has a fever. I'm going to go help her and care for the baby until she feels better."

The next morning Mother was up even before he was. "I made some extra bread," she said. "I put five of them in your little basket, and there are also two fish. Don't eat everything before noon or you'll be really hungry later."

Andrew laughed. His mother knew him pretty well. It just seemed as if he was always hungry these days, but he had grown much taller.

Mother smiled. "You have fun. After all, you've worked hard all week and deserve this. I'll see you tonight."

The boy started off whistling toward Amos's house. His friend and neighbor was interested in Yeshua of Nazareth too. Both Andrew and Amos were certain that He was the Messiah and that He would announce any day now that He would throw the Romans out on their noses. The boys couldn't wait.

Yeshua of Nazareth's sermons were everything that Andrew had hoped they would be. He and Amos listened in fascination and were surprised to realize the day was almost over. Apparently everyone else discovered it about the same time, and suddenly children all through the crowd started crying to their parents for food. It didn't seem that many people had provided for a lunch as Mother had.

Andrew kept his basket under his outer cloak. While it contained five pieces of bread, that was nothing compared to the needs of the crowd. Down front, Yeshua's disciples started asking, "Does anyone have any food? Has anyone brought a lunch? The Master is hungry."

The question made the boy think for a moment. He didn't really want to share His lunch with just anybody, but he would do anything for Yeshua of Nazareth, even give up his food. Pulling it from under his cloak, he said, "I have a lunch. It's just bread and fish, but if the Master would like it, He's most welcome." The boy looked up at the disciple. "You're Andrew, aren't you?"

The bearded man nodded. "Yes, I'm Andrew too. We met before. Come with me, young lad," he said, considerably more friendly than the last time they had encountered each other. The boy followed him down to where Yeshua sat on the huge rock. "This young lad is willing to give You his lunch," he told his Master.

"Why, thank you," the Teacher said. "That is very kind of you, Andrew. God loves a cheerful and willing giver, and He will not forget this."

Blushing, Andrew looked at his feet. "It's only bread and fish."

"Simple food is quite all right," Yeshua of Nazareth told him. "We always ate simply in My home too." He smiled and Andrew felt warm all over. Then Yeshua of Nazareth bowed His head and thanked God for the lunch. Andrew expected Him to start eating, but instead He began tearing apart the flat rounds of bread. As He pulled pieces off them there just seemed to be more and more. He broke the fish and gave some to each disciple. "Have the people sit in groups," He commanded, "and then take the food to them."

The boy couldn't believe his eyes. The more Yeshua broke the food, the more there was. The disciples kept busy carrying basket after basket of bread and fish. And though thousands covered the hillside (5,000 men, not counting the women and children), everyone had enough to eat. Indeed, baskets of it remained left over.

Mother was right. Surely this must be the Messiah! Just think how wonderful it would be to have a King in Jerusalem who could multiply food by just breaking it with His hands. No one in Israel would ever go hungry again.

Andrew was so excited he could hardly contain himself. He couldn't wait to tell his mother all that had happened. She would be delighted to know she was right.

Levi

AT THE TEMPLE IN JERUSALEM

 evi stood at the gate of the outer court of the Temple. He loved Passover. Everyone who worshiped God assembled at Jerusalem for Passover, not just those in Israel, but also people from many neighboring countries and some distant ones. It was an exciting time. Today Levi had received gate duty. It was his responsibility to give directions to the people entering the Temple courts and to help them find what they needed. He had always been an avid people-watcher, and Passover was the perfect time for that. Working the gates enabled him to see everything and everyone.

A family approached him. "May I help you?" he asked.

"Yes," the young father said, "we've brought a lamb for sacrifice, but we're not sure where to go."

"Ah, this must be your first time here."

"Yes," the man said. "We have come to the Passover as . . ."

Levi smiled. "I understand. God will bless you for that. First of all, you need to take your lamb into this courtyard." He pointed. "Over on that side a priest will inspect your lamb. If your lamb is perfect . . ."

"Oh yes, sir. He is perfect. We would only bring the best."

The Levite nodded, remembering as a child bringing his perfect lamb and having the priests reject it, and then seeing it sold as a perfect lamb later for three times the money they had given him. A bitter knot twisted in his chest. *There is nothing I can do about it,* he thought.

"I understand," he said out loud, "but it needs to be inspected by a priest. So that's where you need to go. After that, the priest will instruct you on what you need to do. And the actual sacrifice is done inside the court of Israel. Your women and children can wait in the court of women while you take your sacrifice in."

"Thank you," the young man said, bowing slightly. The women in the group smiled shyly at Levi, and the little family proceeded in. Another young couple approached, carrying a small child. The child's eyes did not look right to Levi. Something was wrong, though he wasn't sure what. Also the child's arms and legs dangled listlessly.

"May I help you?" Levi questioned automatically.

"Oh please, yes," the father began. "Our child is ill. We have come with an offering to the Lord and to pray for his healing."

"You need to go directly to that priest." Levi pointed across the courtyard to the priest at the next gate. "He will direct you to the right place for your sacrifice and help you with the prayers to offer. May God heal your son. He is merciful."

The little family headed in the direction indicated.

The next group that approached looked wealthy. Their clothes were of finer fabric than the homespun wool and rough linen garments that most Jews wore.

Levi looked at him, but before he could offer to help, the man asked, "Are you the one to give directions? Which way do we go to buy a lamb? We want to offer a sacrifice—nothing but the best. Please direct us to the best vendors."

With a laugh Levi swung his arm toward the many vendors in the courtyard. "There's not a seller here that will admit he has anything but the best. You may choose from any of them. Do you have Temple coins?"

The man shook his head. "I have only drachmas."

"Then you need to go to the money changers first and get your money transferred into Temple currency. After you get them, proceed to any of these animal vendors here to purchase your sacrifice."

Dismissing Levi with an abrupt nod, the pilgrim set off toward the money changers. Levi shook his head. He hated the money changers. He was not sure where the custom had come from of requiring only Temple currency for purchasing animals and sacrifices and paying offerings. Pilgrims had to exchange their coins for Tyrian half-shekels. Although they depicted the head of a pagan god, the priests were more interested in the purity and consistent weight of the silver in them. And the exchange provided a golden opportunity for the money changers to cheat everyone coming to the Temple. Though people knew they were being taken advantage of, they had no choice. But surely it was not God's will for His worshipers, who were already giving freely and out of love for Him, to be cheated and leave feeling wounded by the very One they had come to worship.

The noise was deafening in the animal market. The shouting of the money changers and those they were serving, the cries of the animals being sold and awaiting their death as sacrifices, and the vendors shouting the virtues of their wares all blended into a cacophony that numbed the mind.

Shaking his head, Levi turned his back to the noisy courtyard. He loved the Lord of Israel and His Temple and the privilege of serving there as a Levite, but the activities on the boundaries of the Temple site always gave him a bad taste in his mouth and bitterness in his spirit.

Another young man approached him with a small child. "I need to see a priest about an illness," he explained. The child looked intelligent and peered shyly at the Levite. When Levi smiled the little one smiled back.

"He looks like a bright child," Levi commented. "I am sure the Lord will heal him. First you need to purchase a sacrifice."

"We have no money," the young man sighed.

"I see. The priest who diagnoses illnesses and offers prayers for healing is right over there. Take your little one to him and explain to him about your financial situation. Our God is a God of mercy who loves the poor and rich alike."

"So they say," the young father muttered with more than a trace of bitterness in his voice.

Levi suddenly stared at him. "Have I met you before? You look familiar."

"Probably. Our country is not a large one, and we all assemble here in the Temple four times a year when we are being devout." He grimaced, then blurted, "My name is David. I am from Bethlehem."

"Ah. Well, I wish the best for your son."

"It's not my son," David hissed. "It's me. And now I will see the priest if you will excuse me." Abruptly he headed toward the priest that Levi had pointed out to him.

Again Levi shook his head. The Lord did love the poor as well as the wealthy; he was sure of it. Why else would He have given separate rules so that those who could not afford to offer a lamb to ransom their firstborn could substitute two pigeons? Surely the young man could still offer prayers for healing even if he could not purchase a sacrificial animal.

It seemed only moments before the young man strode back out the gate at a furious pace.

"David," Levi called after him. "David, what did the priest say?"

The supplicant turned to him, eyes blazing with fury. "The priest says I have leprosy and that I am unclean and am banished from civilization."

The blood drained from the Levite's face. "I am sorry. What about the boy?"

"I asked if the priest could keep him here at the Temple like young Samuel in the stories we've been told. But they have no interest in a young boy because I have no money to offer them for his keep, and am unlikely to come across any as a leper." He spat the word out.

"What will you do?" Levi continued. "Do you have a wife? family? What about your parents?"

"I have no family." Anger tinged his words. "My father disappeared when I was very young, and my mother died shortly after Herod had the children killed in Bethlehem—one of his final crimes before he finally died. Would that he could have died a little earlier, for his soldiers killed my little brother, and my mother died of grief only days afterward."

The young man's grief and almost palpable bitterness overwhelmed Levi.

"I will take Jonathan with me," David spat. "Perhaps he is better off in a colony of rotting lepers with a father who cares for him than in a place like this with these so-called servants of God who care for no one." Then he disappeared into the crowd.

Levi felt the same old confusion creeping back into his mind. He had served at the gate next to the priest and watched him diagnosing leprosy. Occasionally worshipers with large amounts of money slipped them to the priest in addition to the required offering. They received a bill of good health even though they had obvious scaly white patches on them, whereas poor worshipers who might not actually even have leprosy found themselves banished with the dreaded diagnosis. Surely it was not God's plan that such a serious procedure as determining leprosy would depend on the bribe one could afford. How could God allow this, right in the courts of His house, His Temple? Could it be that God was that way too? That seemed to be David's understanding. Angrily Levi shook his head. "No," he said to himself, "I just can't believe that God would do that."

Levi continued to serve at the gate and instruct the hundreds of people pouring in and out of the Temple grounds. A small group of young men came through, apparently unmarried or too poor to bring their families along. They did not have a sacrifice with them, so he directed them to the vendors. They obediently headed toward them.

Another vendor had come through a few minutes before with a new herd of lambs. And the Temple servant in charge of cleaning up had not made it back to Levi's gate yet. "Excuse me, sir," he said as another man entered, "watch where you . . . never mind," he mumbled as the man swore and tried to clean his sandal off on the steps.

"This is disgusting," the Temple visitor said. "I can't believe I stepped in this right on the steps going up to the house of the Lord."

Just as Levi started to apologize the usual roar of the Temple grounds suddenly swelled into a deafening panic. Levi heard the crash of tables overturning and the ping of coins hitting the pavement stones. People and animals screamed in terror. Above it all, he heard Someone's voice. "My Father's house should be a house of prayer. You have turned it into a marketplace and a den of thieves. How can you cheat people in the very presence of My Father?"

The money changers fled, almost knocking Levi to the ground as they hurried out. "And you," the Man who had started the turmoil said, pointing at the priest in charge of prayers for the sick.

The priest turned deathly pale. The small bag of coins he had hidden in his robe fell and scattered on the paving stones as he turned and ran. Levi pressed into the court so he could see more clearly. Priests fled in fear in every direction. The vendors ran too. The animals, without anyone on the other end of their ropes, wandered around bleating and mooing, soon heading for the gates. Yet the worshipers continued to crowd into the Temple courtyard.

Edging closer, Levi wanted to see more of the One who had triggered the commotion. He smiled. The Man had the courage to say out loud what Levi had always kept to himself. He must be a good man. Now the Stranger was talking to the family who had the sick child that Levi had noticed earlier. Gently He lifted the boy from the father's arms and held him for a moment. Then the little one's arms suddenly twitched with life, and instead of hanging limply, pulled up to his chest. With one hand he reached up and touched his Healer on the face.

Levi pushed his way closer. The eyes that hadn't seemed to focus before were now clear and healthy and concentrating on the Man holding him. The child let out a little giggle, and the Man handed him back to his father.

The father was speechless, but the mother burst into tears. "He's been healed! He's never been like this since he was born. Oh, thank you. Oh, praise God! Who are you?" she asked.

The Man just smiled at her. "Praise God," He said. "Thank Him, for all life and all good things come from Him."

Then He spoke to other families, explaining to them that the Almighty never intended to cheat them, but welcomed their offerings in love as small tokens in response to the love and gifts He had to pour out on them.

Surely this is the best thing that has ever happened at our Temple in my entire lifetime, Levi thought. *But I wonder how the priests are going to react to this.* At the time, though, Levi didn't care. He just wanted to get as close to the Man as he could.

Samuel

amuel stood as tall as he could on the banks of the Jordan, his legs spread wide apart, his hands clasped behind his back. He hoped he looked dignified and important. After all, his job was truly important. Father had gone back to his position at the palace of King Herod and had given Samuel some money and allowed him to stay and tend to the needs of the Baptist.

"Many of his disciples are very poor," his father had explained, "and we are not. The steward of the palace pays me well for what I do, and I am happy to provide for John's needs. You remain here and keep an eye on him. He has many enemies, you know."

Samuel had come to love the sharp-tongued preacher and agreed with him that it was time for people to turn back to God, especially since the Messiah was somewhere in the land. It was no time for people to cling to cherished sins.

Now the young man watched as John paused from his preaching and backed into the river to baptize more disciples into its depths. He frowned as he thought of the argument he had had with his cousin, Andrew, the night before. His cousin lived up in a fishing village in Galilee, but they had gotten to see each other during the Passover. Samuel kicked the ground in frustration. Andrew was now following the young Teacher they had been hearing so many things about. Apparently the Man was a cousin of the Baptist, although they had not met except for His baptism some time before.

Suddenly Samuel scowled to himself. If he had come to the Baptist for baptism, then surely He was subordinate to the Baptist and should teach His followers more respect, yet His disciples seemed to believe that He was the Messiah and that the Baptist was of less importance. Even more distressing was the fact that the crowds flocking to the Jordan were smaller than they had been. The crowds that Andrew described as following Yeshua grew daily and now outnumbered the dwindling Jordan group.

It's not right, Samuel thought. *He's stealing disciples from the Baptist.* He decided to speak with John about it later. In fact, he needed to talk with him anyway, for Father was very concerned. In his denouncing of sin, the preacher had also attacked the sins of the country's leadership. Condemning the sins of a Roman governor did not shock anyone, but calling the priests and rabbis "vipers" and "whitewashed sepulchers" were serious insults. He was making powerful enemies. Even worse, he had accused Herod Antipas, the ruler of the territory he preached in. Of course, Antipas had had a flagrant affair with his brother's wife, divorcing his own wife to marry Herodias. But the preacher could have used a little more tact. Like his infamous father, this Herod was not known for taking criticism well, and the Baptist ignored tact when it came to pointing out sin. Father said that word had gotten back to Antipas, leaving him furious.

Samuel continued to watch the crowd. Father had worked in Herod's court many years, and Samuel recognized the faces not only of the palace servants, but also of the ruler's favorite agents whom he sent out on spying missions. Already Samuel had seen some of them several times. He had warned John about this before, but they were showing up on a daily basis now, increasing Father's concern. *I'll have to talk to him tonight for sure,* the young man thought.

That evening, as the crowds dispersed to their homes and darkness set in, the Baptist sat near the fire Samuel had prepared. "Your lentil stew is delicious," the preacher said. "Thank you so much, Samuel. This is quite an improvement on the years of locusts and honey."

The boy laughed. "I can't imagine living on that stuff."

John smiled. "It filled my stomach and kept me alive. I had more important things to think about, but I do appreciate a good lentil stew and fresh bread. Where did you get it?"

"I bought it in the village."

"You seem quite well provided for," the preacher observed.

"I've been meaning to talk to you about this. My father serves in Herod's palace. He provided the dinner I bought and the other things."

"Ah, that's a good thing. I would much rather have you the son of a rich servant than a young thief who steals pots of lentil stew in order to feed your favorite preacher." They laughed.

"I must talk to you, rabbi."

"Don't call me rabbi. You know that no self-respecting rabbi would like to be considered in the same class as me." It was true, but Samuel didn't want to agree with him, for he had more respect for the Baptist than any rabbi he had ever met.

"The spies from the palace are turning up here more often," he continued. "Father says that Herod has heard of the things you have said about his wife."

John snorted.

"You have to stop saying such things about them. He's getting really angry."

The Baptist turned his steady gaze from the fire to Samuel. "I don't have to stop anything," he said. "I am making the way ready for the Messiah, and I have been sent to point out sin wherever it is. As long as the country's leaders are wallowing in their sins, God cannot bless the country. It's always been that way. Remember the stories of Ahab? Herod is no different. Unless he is willing to put away his sin and stop his evil behavior with her who should be his brother's wife, I will not stop denouncing him."

Taking a breath, Samuel tried a different tactic. "Father says that a few days ago Herod, after hearing the spies reporting on your comments, said that if you didn't stop he was going to have them bring you in and make you say it to his face."

John looked at him unblinking. "I would do that. I would not say anything differently behind a man's back than I would tell him to his face."

Samuel sighed. One thing you could say for the Baptist was that he was straightforward and took the same position no matter who was listening. "Please be careful," the young man begged. "I have grown to respect you and care for you very much, and it would sadden me if anything happened to you."

The Baptist laughed. "Nothing will happen to me that the Lord doesn't allow, so don't worry."

Shaking his head, Samuel wished he had the confidence that the Baptist had, but all he felt was a growing, gnawing fear inside him.

"Is there anything else on your mind?" the preacher asked as he ladled a second bowl of the savory stew.

"Yes. It's about that other young Preacher, the One you baptized. His name is Yeshua."

"Yes, my cousin."

"Have you noticed that He's drawing such crowds that we are now losing disciples to Him? You used to have lots more, and now many of them have left us to follow Him."

John nodded and finished chewing the mouthful he had. "None of us have a following except that God impresses people to listen. If Yeshua has more followers than me, it's because God wants it that way. And if my disciples are leaving me to follow Him, then that is also the plan of the Almighty, and I approve."

"But, but," Samuel sputtered, "it's not fair. You've been preaching longer than He has. *You* baptized Him. You should be the more important one."

The Baptist stared into the fire for a long time and then shook his head and turned to Samuel. "Not necessarily. At a wedding the groom is delighted over his pretty bride. And friends of the groom should delight over his happiness and not be jealous of it. As time goes on now, Yeshua will increase in popularity. His crowds will get bigger and His reputation will become even more widespread than it is now."

"But what about you?"

"I guess I will decrease as He increases. I don't know. The Almighty has not revealed to me what His plans for me are. I just know I was here to prepare the way for Yeshua's ministry—for the Messiah."

"He's the Messiah?"

John set down his bowl. "I think so. No, I am certain of it. And once the way is prepared and people abandon their sin and follow Him, perhaps He will overthrow the Romans. Whatever kingdom He sets up, it is the will of the Almighty. Perhaps then He and I will get together and be able to be the close cousins you and Andrew—as I always wished we could have been."

"You were never close?"

"No. His parents were very poor and lived in Nazareth. My parents were more prosperous, but were old and ill and could not travel. We knew of each other yet we have never spent any time together as families. I hope someday to do that."

Although Samuel nodded, he hoped in his heart that they wouldn't. Hating the young Preacher who had lured so many disciples away from the Baptist, he wished that Yeshua would make some political mistakes and that His followers would return to the Baptist.

Antonia

I always enjoyed my assignments in Capernaum, for the Son of the Most High came through here frequently on His journeys. Partly because it was on his way, partly because several of his closest friends had been born in Capernaum. The noisy Zebedee brothers had a home in the town. During this assignment I was with a girl named Antonia. Antonia was not a Jew, but the daughter of a Roman centurion stationed in Capernaum with his garrison of men to maintain law and order. Her father was not like most centurions, and that fact made my job more enjoyable.

Antonia carried the platter of fruit in and set it on the table for her father and his friends, who were laughing and talking. "So, Longenius," her father said, "rumor has it that you and Brutus went to see the Baptist in the wilderness. What did you think?"

The laughing stopped. Brutus and Longenius became serious. "It's true," Brutus replied, "that we went."

"So what did you find?"

"We can count on you," Longenius stated, "to keep everything we say within these walls?"

Father nodded, then smiled at Antonia as she set the platter down. "And she can be trusted. She has been raised to be the daughter of a centurion." The girl smiled as she filled their cups.

"We were baptized," Longenius announced after a pause.

"You were what?" Father dropped his cup on the floor.

"He preached so powerfully of the coming of Judea's Messiah. He said it was time to prepare the way of their Lord."

Father studied his fingernails for some time and then looked at Longenius. "I have thought for some time," he said, "that we would be wise to treat the Judean God with a little respect."

"And you know we Romans are known for treating their God with as little respect as possible," Brutus laughed.

They all laughed. Then their leader continued, "No, seriously, I have donated money for them to build a synagogue for Him here in Capernaum. The more I learn of His ways, the more I think He must be a very just and fair God and there may be something to this Judean religion."

Brutus let out a sigh of relief. "We thought you might think we were traitors to the emperor, because the Judeans believe that when the Messiah comes, He will expel us."

"Of course, if He did," Longenius joked, "it would be helpful to have some friends in His camp, since we would not be their favorite people."

The centurion frowned. "All this Messiah talk leaves me very confused. While I really am impressed with some aspects of the Judean God, I can't imagine this Yeshua of Nazareth doing a military coup. He does not strike me as that type of person."

"You've met Him?" Longenius asked.

"Yes, He comes to Capernaum quite frequently. Two of His followers are from this town, and so we have had Him under surveillance from the beginning. I believe He's the one whom your Baptist identified as the Messiah."

"Why didn't you tell us?" Brutus inquired.

Their commander laughed nervously. "I guess for the same reason that you have waited all this time to tell me that you were baptized."

Antonia listened eagerly. Her best friend was a Judean, a young girl named Deborah. Deborah's father was highly placed in Jewish society, so it was not lowering herself to be friends with her. Both Antonia and Deborah were used to having servants. Deborah's father frowned on both the followers of the Baptist and those of Yeshua of Nazareth. He often said that both were just trying to stir the people up and make trouble when things were working as well as they could under the circumstances.

When Antonia returned to the kitchen with the empty wine jug, Petronius was there speaking with the house servants and outlining their duties for the next day. Pain seemed to have lined his face, and he looked ill. As soon as he finished and the servants left for their tasks, she asked, "What is the matter, Petronius?"

"I don't know. I've had a headache all day."

"Sit down. Let me give you something to drink. You've been working too hard."

Although Petronius was her father's chief steward, he seemed more like a second father to Antonia. Being a centurion, her father often had to leave her when his garrison reported for duty elsewhere. Petronius had watched over her and made sure that she was safe and happy ever since her mother had died when she was very young.

She poured him a cup of wine and brought a wet cloth to place on his forehead. "I worry about you. You've been having headaches more and more often."

"Yes, and they seem to be getting worse. Several times this afternoon I felt as if my arm and my leg on this side were tingling or even numb. I'm not sure what is happening, but I wish it would go away."

"Perhaps we should call a doctor," Antonia suggested. "There is a Greek one not too far from here."

"I know," Petronius said. "These silly Jews think that all illness is a curse from their God. So doctors are hard to find here, because who wants to cure something that their God wants them to have in the first place? I'm grateful we have a few Greeks and Romans around so that we can get medical care when we need it."

"Would you like me to send someone to fetch the doctor?"

"No, not yet. Likely as not, they'll think I have spirits in my head that need letting out, and start drilling holes in it. It may have helped other people, but I don't feel bad enough to let them do that to me yet."

The girl laughed. "I don't blame you for that. Why don't you lie down and have a rest?"

"No, I can't do that. There's still much to do. Your father and his friends will soon be finished with their dinner, and there are plans I need to discuss with your father for this week before he goes off on another trip."

Antonia frowned. "Well, at least rest until they're done eating. I don't want anything to happen to you."

His gaze softened as he looked at her. "We've been together a long time, Antonia. I would not like anything bad to happen to you, either. We'll just stick together no matter what."

She smiled. "I'll go back and check on Father and his friends and see if they need anything else." Turning, she headed back toward the room where her father and his friends were eating.

As he started to enter the dining chamber, Petronius reached his hand out to steady himself against the wall, wobbled for a moment, and then slowly slid to the floor. He tried to open his mouth to call for help, but his tongue felt as if it had swollen to the size of his foot, and all that came out was a gurgling, croaking sound. Then all became darkness.

* * *

"Papa, please do something to help him," Antonia sobbed. "Surely there must be something we can do." The three soldiers stood helplessly as servants bustled around lifting Petronius from the floor and placing him on a mat. They propped him on pillows and wiped his face. He opened his eyes.

"Look, he's awake," the girl cried.

"Petronius," Father said, "we've been worried about you."

The servant's gaze lifted from Antonia to her father. He opened his mouth, but only a grunt came out.

"Are you able to speak?" Father asked.

Petronius groaned again. He tried to move one hand and was able to gesture a little; then it fell weakly to his side. The other hand just lay limp on the coverlet. Antonia noticed that one side of his face sagged and drooped. That side of his mouth didn't seem able to move either.

"What is it, Father?" she asked. "Is it something that can be helped by the physicians? Are there herbs to ease this type of problem?"

Her father shook his head. "I don't think so, Antonia. We've seen this before, and it's not good."

She tried to give Petronius a sip of water, but he choked. Quickly the three men rolled him on his side so that the water trickled out of his mouth instead of gagging him.

"I don't think he can swallow, Antonia. I don't think you should try that again."

"But if he can't swallow, how will we feed him?" Father just shook his head.

"Oh, Petronius," she cried, and fell on her knees with her head on his chest. The three men conferred quietly among themselves.

"Well," Brutus said finally, "either we believe in this Healer or we don't."

"What do you mean?" Father asked.

"Well, if we believe that the Baptist is right, then this Man is the Judean Messiah. We've heard that He does healings for His fellow Judeans. Perhaps if we ask Him . . ."

"We can't ask Him," Father observed. "We're Romans. They hate us."

"I don't know," Longenius commented. "This Man seems different, although I'm sure a good share of His followers hate us."

"But it won't hurt to ask," Brutus said. "So what if He says no? Surely someone has said no to you before."

Father looked at him. "Do you think He would heal the servant of a Roman?"

"I don't know," Brutus replied.

"Perhaps you should send some of the Jewish elders from Capernaum," Longenius suggested. "After all, you did build a synagogue for them. I'm sure if the elders explained to Yeshua of Nazareth how tolerant you have been toward them and how you have actually helped them practice their religion, He might be more sympathetic."

"Excellent plan," Father agreed. "I will send a servant to the elders right away and get someone on the road to Yeshua."

Antonia lifted her tear-stained face and looked at her father. "Please send him immediately."

"I don't know if this is going to help, Antonia. Don't get your hopes up. He may be the Judean Messiah, but we are only Romans. I won't ask Him to come here. As the Messiah He presumably would have authority to command a healing by just speaking."

"You think so?" his daughter asked.

"If He's who He seems to be, then He should be able to, and we are not important enough to summon Him to our home. I shouldn't have sent the elders to ask Yeshua to come here. It could get Him in a lot of trouble having contact with us Romans, and I'm sure He doesn't need any more political problems than He's got already. I must send some servants to ask Him just to speak the word and my servant will be healed. I'm sure He can do that."

Antonia's father continued to mumble to himself. "Surely if I, a centurion, can just speak the word from Capernaum and have my wishes taken care of, He, the Messiah, can do the same."

"I will stay here with Petronius," Antonia announced. "It's going to be all right," she whispered to him. "They say that Yeshua of Nazareth has healed a lot of people, and I know He can heal you too."

But the elderly servant seemed to have drifted back to sleep.

* * *

As Antonia knelt next to Petronius she wiped his face with a damp cloth. The old servant made a little choking noise. "Here, let me help you," Longenius offered. "If you turn him on his side, then he can drool out the corner of his mouth and won't choke on his own saliva." Gently the young girl and the burly soldier shifted the older man. She positioned a clean cloth under the servant's face to catch the forming puddle.

Father began pacing the floor, something he did whenever he felt powerless. It was an unusual feeling for a centurion, and though it happened occasionally, it always left him frustrated. Brutus and Longenius had known him long enough to recognize his behavior and to stay out of the way. Reclining on one of the dining couches, Brutus nervously munched one piece of dried fruit after another and became more annoyed by the moment.

"Stop it!" he snapped at last.

Glancing in his direction, Father grumbled, "Brutus, if you keep stuffing yourself we will have to send a message to the Galilean Healer for you, too." Then frowning, he resumed pacing. Longenius glanced at Brutus; then the two friends sighed. It was going to be a long day.

"I should have gone myself with my servants," Father muttered to himself.

Pausing between mouthfuls of figs, Brutus interrupted, "If this Yeshua really heals Petronius, then what are we going to do?"

"If He heals Petronius, then we believe in Him," Father answered slowly. "He obviously has powers beyond that of any ordinary man."

"But there is a problem with that," Brutus said cautiously. "We believe in many gods, so adding this Judean Messiah to the list is no problem to us, but the Judeans believe in only one God. They say He will not let people worship anyone else. How do we know if this

Messiah won't be the same way? If He heals Petronius, what are we going to do about it? To be a Roman and to worship the empire's gods are inseparable. You know how our religion touches every aspect of our lives."

"I don't know," Father groaned. "I just don't know. But if this man is really the Judean Messiah, He will have to show us."

Petronius moaned and swallowed.

"Shh!" Antonia scolded as she wiped his face again.

Just then the old servant blinked and sat up. "I must have been sleeping," he muttered. As he glanced around an expression of horror crossed his face. "I have been sleeping in the dining hall!" he exclaimed in disbelief as he jumped to his feet. "I beg you pardon, miss, sirs."

Squealing with delight, the girl flung her arms around his neck. "You are healed! You are healed! Yeshua of Nazareth has healed you. Oh, wait till I tell Deborah." The three soldiers stood there grinning elatedly and nodding. When they had convinced Petronius that he had been unconscious and near death, the servant sank onto one of the couches and allowed them to bring him something to eat and drink.

A few minutes later Brutus asked, "Do you think this Yeshua really healed him, or did Petronius just recover on his own?" Father, Longenius, and Antonia frowned at him.

"Of course Yeshua did it," the girl exploded. "My father asked Him, didn't he?"

"Don't look to me for answers," Petronius said, shaking his head. "I can't remember a thing except that I had a terrible headache and then woke up in here."

A shadow filled the doorway. Antonia glanced toward it and exclaimed, "Look, here is Deborah. Come in! You won't believe what has happened here."

"Please come outside," Deborah said quietly.

Realizing that her friend felt uncomfortable in a Roman home, Antonia said, "Father, Deborah and I will be in the courtyard if you need us."

Father nodded. Then before they could leave, he asked Deborah, "Is your father back?"

The girl bowed her head. "Yes. Father said that Yeshua was not upset at all that you were Roman. He said your Petronius would be healed. Then when your servants arrived and told Him that Yeshua didn't have to come, that He could just say the word, He really shocked everyone. He said that He had not seen such faith even in Israel."

"Faith?" Father echoed, frowning.

The girl glanced at the centurion's face. "My father frowned like that too."

"I'll bet he did," Brutus commented, then became silent as Father glared at him.

"Your servants will be back any moment," Deborah continued, "and you can find out more from them." She and Antonia scampered outside.

"This is really awkward for my father," Deborah stated when the two girls reached the courtyard. "He doesn't fully believe in Yeshua, but asked the favor out of gratitude for your father's help in building our synagogue."

"I know," Antonia replied. "It's awkward for my father, too. Romans don't ask favors of anyone. At least usually we don't have to. Still, it was worth it to have Petronius back. I don't know what I'd do without him. Do you really think this Yeshua could be your people's divine leader?"

A look of anger flashed across Deborah's face. "What would Romans know of our God?" she spat out.

Her Roman friend's face flushed. "Well, nothing. That's why I'm asking. If Yeshua is your Messiah, would your God want something from us in return?"

Deborah was quiet for a moment. "I'm sorry. I don't know—I just don't know. But if our God wants us to find out, He'll make a way, and we'll know what to do." Then she added under her breath, "I'm not sure about Romans, though."

ANDREW

NAIN

drew a deep breath. Being a recording angel can be a lot of fun, but on days like this it definitely was not. I had been recording Andrew all of his short life. When he had returned from hearing Yeshua of Nazareth preach, his mother was still helping the sick neighbor woman. The fever had spread to Andrew's mother, and Andrew caught it from her. But while she had recovered, Andrew had grown worse. His young body burned with fever as he tossed to and fro, mumbling all night. By the next afternoon he was dead.

His mother's sorrow was uncontrollable. He had been everything that she had left. Now I walked beside her as they carried him to his final resting place. He lay on the open bier carried by four of the village young men. Behind him walked his mother and then the other members of the funeral party. The mourning was loud and sincere. His mother had lost her only son, the only man she was related to apart from her unkind uncle who lived several miles away.

Until now she had been able to remain in her dead husband's home that her son would inherit. Now it was no longer hers, for a woman without a husband or a son had no value.

As the funeral procession reached the outskirts of the village and headed down the hill toward the cemetery, I saw Yeshua, the human Son of the Almighty, and His group of disciples coming from the other direction. Just to be in His presence filled me with joy. Perhaps today would not be so bad after all.

As the funeral party approached, the disciples stepped off the path. It was taboo to touch a dead body, and none of them wanted to be made unclean by it. But Yeshua seemed not to notice. He walked right up to the bier and looked.

The pallbearers paused and set it down for Him to see. He recognized the young lad immediately. Peter and Andrew and their friend, John, stepped up behind Yeshua.

"Look," Peter said, "it's the little boy with the lunch."

"Yes, with my name," Andrew added.

Yeshua nodded. He turned to the boy's mother. "Your son?" He asked.

The disciples frowned. Respectable Jewish men did not speak to women who were not a blood relative or a wife. Yeshua always seemed to be forgetting these things. Now He broke another taboo in front of everyone as He reached out and touched the boy.

Andrew put his hand over his face. He had great respect for Yeshua of Nazareth, but his Master's forgetfulness when it came to manners was just unbearable at times. Hearing the murmurs of the crowd, he drew his hands back from his eyes and looked.

The young lad now sat up on the funeral bier, looking confused. "What happened?" he asked.

"My son, my son," his mother screamed, flinging herself on him and covering him with hugs and kisses.

Yeshua smiled. The mourners stopped their wailing and started shouting with delight. Then everybody made their way back toward the village. I smiled. Everywhere Yeshua went He restored the value of those He came in contact with and affirmed them, leaving them feeling loved and treasured by the Almighty. Today was not going to be a bad day after all.

Antonia

CAPERNAUM

eborah, Deborah," Antonia called.

"What is it?" asked the young Jewish girl.

"I saw the weirdest thing last night," Antonia exclaimed. "I was on top of our house looking out across the Sea of Galilee . . ."

"You were on top of your house," Deborah echoed in disbelief, "during that horrible storm?"

"Yes. Father hates it when I go up there during storms, but I just love the wind. Yesterday that young Preacher and His friends left from here in a boat."

"I was out listening to Him preach," Deborah interrupted. "It was wonderful. Where did they go?"

"Well, it was the strangest thing. They just got a little way out before the storm blew in. It was a violent one. The wind swept down from the mountains, and the waves were high and rough. The little boat was tossing about like a twig on the rough waters."

"Your father would be upset with you for being up there in a storm like that," Deborah protested. "Some debris could have hit you, or you could have been blown off the roof."

"I felt safe enough, but Yeshua's disciples must have been panic-stricken. They were trying to bale and row. I couldn't see very well, but I thought they were going to drown."

Deborah shuddered. "Well, I've seen boats go down in the lake before during these storms. I hope Yeshua's didn't. The Teacher has quite a following. Many would be sad if anything happened to Him."

"That's the point," Antonia continued. "Someone—I think it was Him—stood up in the boat and stretched his arms out, and immediately the storm ceased right in the middle of the crashing and the thundering and the waves! Everything stopped, the lake became as smooth as a mirror, and the one who had stood up just continued standing there in the boat. Who in their right mind would stand up in a boat when it was that rough?"

Deborah smiled. "I've heard a lot of things like that about Him. Besides healing people, He can turn water into wine."

"Well, after what I saw last night, I would believe anything about Him. I hope He comes back. After seeing that, I would really like to hear what He has to say."

"I hope He will too. I'm sure He wouldn't mind if you came and listened, although He is one of my people."

Antonia laughed. "Well, He may be a Jew, but we Romans can do anything we want here."

The Galilean girl looked at the ground and said nothing.

"I'm sorry," said Antonia. "Look, you're my best friend, and I don't even mind if you're a Jew. I just wish Yeshua of Nazareth would come back."

Deborah nodded. "So do I. Antonia, I really don't feel well; I think I'm getting a fever or something. I need to go lie down."

"Here, I'll walk you home."

* * *

"Dead! How can she be dead! I was talking to her just yester-day," Antonia sobbed.

Petronius put his arm around his little mistress. "Her mother says she fell ill sometime yesterday. Was she well when you were talking with her?"

"She did complain of a headache and said she needed to go home and lie down."

"Her mother says this morning they were unable to wake her up, but she was still breathing. Her father Jairus set out immediately to find Yeshua of Nazareth, hoping that He could heal her. A few minutes ago she stopped breathing. They have sent a servant to let Jairus know not to bother the Rabbi and to come home and help with funeral preparations."

Antonia burst into tears. *This can't be happening,* she thought. She pulled on her outdoor cloak. "Petronius, I am going over to Deborah's house to see if they will let me mourn with them," she called over her shoulder.

* * *

"Petronius! You won't believe what has just happened!" Antonia shouted as she raced toward the house sometime later.

"Why are you so excited?" the servant asked, setting an amphora of wine down.

"Deborah is alive!"

It took a moment for her words to register. "They were mistaken about her breathing, then? I know sometimes when people are ill their breathing gets so shallow that people think . . ."

"No, Deborah was really dead. The servant reached Jairus just after Jairus got to Yeshua. Yeshua kept heading toward Capernaum anyway. He stopped to heal a woman who had been bleeding for years and years, but that's another story, though it proves what Deborah said about her God, and . . ."

"Stop! Stop! Take a breath!" Petronius laughed. "One sentence at a time. I am an old man. You are confusing me. Tell me about Deborah."

"Yeshua of Nazareth arrived at the house and told all the mourners to go outside. He took just Deborah's parents into her room. In minutes they came out with her—and she was starving! They fed her fruit and bread, and she drank and everything. Definitely not dead!" Antonia chortled with delight.

"How long will it take for people to realize who He is and make Him their king?" Petronius wondered out loud—and then looked anxiously around to make sure someone hadn't overheard him.

"I don't know," answered Antonia, "but I hope it is soon."

THAD

GADARA

 had trudged up the hill holding the basket of food. He hated this task. Every day Mother would pack a lunch and he would carry it up toward the cemetery. It wasn't the cemetery that made him nervous. It was his father.

His friend, Nathan, told him he should be glad his father was alive at least, for Nathan's father had died in one of the storms out on the lake. Thad secretly thought, though, that he would prefer his father to have died than to end up like this. He reached the edge of the cemetery.

"Hello," he called in a small voice. "Hello."

Two men came screaming out from behind the rocks. Their hair matted, they were naked and filthy and covered with sores. Worst of all, they were insane. Thad dropped the food and ran. The two men pounced on the little basket and began clawing and shoving food into their mouths like wild animals.

Thad knew they were hungry. Not only did he fear being near them, but it also made him feel sick in the pit of his stomach to see the emaciated, wild man his gentle father had become. Mother said he had had a fever and just never recovered, but the elder in the synagogue said that he had a demon. The boy didn't know what to think, but more and more it seemed that his father was truly turning into a demon—if such a thing was possible. Surely even if Father died it would be less difficult than to see him this way.

As Thad sped down the hill from the cemetery he rounded the corner by the lake and ran into a small group of men walking up the path. "Will you watch where you're going?" one man complained as he and Thad both picked themselves up. The other men just laughed.

Someone grabbed Thad's hand and pulled him back to his feet. "Don't listen to him. He's just a Zebedee. Those sons of thunder are always thundering about something," he said.

The rest laughed again. Thad looked from face to face. "What are you running from?" asked the One in the middle.

"Uh, the cemetery." Thad pointed. "Back there."

"What could have frightened you so badly in the cemetery?" they asked.

Thad frantically searched for words. Should he tell them? Or should he make something up? "There are two demoniacs up there," he said. "They came screaming out from the caves and chased me."

"Let's go see," the One in the middle said, starting on His way.

"No, let's not," protested the one Thad had knocked over. But the One in the middle was already walking briskly up the path. Thad counted quickly. Thirteen men. They should be able to handle the two demoniacs without any problem. He decided to follow. Sure enough, the two had finished devouring the lunch. They had ripped the wrapping cloth to shreds, and the basket lay broken in pieces on the path.

The Man in front turned around and looked at Thad. "You brought them food."

As the boy stared at his feet the Man in front just smiled, as if He already knew and understood. Saying nothing, Thad scuffed his toe in the dust.

"I am Yeshua, and your name is . . ."

"Thaddeus, but everyone just calls me Thad."

Yeshua nodded. "Come with Me, Thad, and don't be afraid. Everything's going to be all right."

Timidly Thad followed. Suddenly horrible screams slashed the air. Unable to help it, the boy bolted back down the hillside.

I smiled. Thad had no reason to be afraid. While demoniacs could be dangerous, demons could do nothing in the presence of the Son of the Almighty. Yeshua said a few words to the two friends closest to Him, and they ran down the path after Thad, quickly catching up with him. "Thaddeus, wait."

The boy stopped. Surely the men weren't going to drag him back up and make him face his father. "Thad, wait. Don't be afraid. The Master says that you should go back home and bring two sets of garments, one for your father and one for his friend."

The boy just stared at them. "How did you know he was my father?"

"We didn't know. The Master told us. My name is James and this is John, my brother—yes, the sons of thunder. If you think we're noisy, you should hear our father on a bad day."

The two men laughed. "Now go back to town as quickly as you can and get some clothing for those two men. It's obvious Yeshua has plans for them."

"But—but," Thad protested. "They tear everything to shreds. They're crazy."

"They seem to be, but if Yeshua said to do that, you might as well do what He said, because He's very persistent and He can do miracles. There's no telling what's happening up there on the hill now. We want to go back and see. You go get the clothes."

"I will," the boy shouted over his shoulder. A little flicker of hope gave wings to his feet. He ran all the way back into the village. Quickly he flung open the basket in the corner of their tiny house and pulled out two of the robes he could remember his father wearing back in better times. Rummaging around, he found two undergarments and a pair of sandals. Wrapping them all in a bundle, he turned and raced back up the path. When he reached the cemetery, his mouth dropped open as he stood panting and staring.

Yeshua of Nazareth stood in His underclothing, His outer robe wrapped around Thad's father. Another one of Yeshua's friends was also sitting there in only a loincloth, looking extremely uncomfortable and self-conscious. "Ah, here he is," Yeshua said, seeing the boy. "Sir, your son, Thad, has brought you some clothes of your own."

In the time that it had taken Thad to reach the village and run back up the hill to the cemetery, Yeshua had apparently helped his father and friend wash in the lake. They looked much better. They returned the clothing to Yeshua and His friend and put on their own. While Thad continued to watch in amazement, Yeshua said, "This is your son, Thad. Remember Thaddeus?"

Father glanced around, and then it was his turn to stare. "Thad? Baby Thad?"

The boy started to cry in spite of himself. "I'm not a baby anymore," he said. "I'm 14."

"What happened?" his father asked. "Oh, Thad, how did you get so tall?"

He flung his arms around his son, who hugged him back and sobbed, "I'm not a baby; I'm a man now. You've—you've been gone a long time."

"What happened?" his father repeated.

"You had a demon," said one of Yeshua's friends. "Both of you were demon-possessed. Yeshua cast the demons out."

Thad's father bowed before Yeshua. "Please come to the village so that we can have a feast for You and let everyone know what You did!"

The Teacher shook his head slowly. "No, we will not be welcome in the village. Over there on the hilltop was a very large herd of swine a few minutes ago."

The two former demoniacs glanced in the hilltop's direction. It was empty. "Yes," Thad's father said. "A Gentile estate raises pigs there."

"Well, not anymore," one of Yeshua's disciples laughed.

"What did you do with the swine?" Thad knew that the whole economy of the predominantly Gentile village involved raising and selling pigs.

"You missed it," James told him. "The demons didn't want to leave the men, and asked Yeshua if they could compromise by going into the pigs. Yeshua said they could, but when He cast them out and they entered the pigs, the beasts all jumped right off the cliff into the lake there."

"Every single one of them?" the boy asked in amazement.

"Every single one."

Thad bit his lip. How would the village respond? Would they be glad to see his father and the other man back, or would they be furious about the loss of the herd?

Yeshua, seeming to read the questions in his eyes, said, "One man is worth more than a thousand pigs to God."

To him, too, Thad reminded himself. Not caring what happened in the village, he was glad to have his father back.

"Let us follow You and be Your disciples," Thad's father begged.

Yeshua shook his head. "No, God has a plan for everyone, and His plan for you is to return to your village sane, whole, and healthy. Just go back and tell them what God has done for you, and you will be a greater witness than if you had come with Me and been one of My disciples."

One of Yeshua's friends had a questioning look on his face. I chuckled as I imagined what he was thinking *What? More important than us?* But Yeshua said nothing. He just smiled. Then He faced Thad. "You too. You have been a faithful son, good to your mother and good and loyal to your father in spite of his illness. Now your family is restored, but I need you to tell people in your village what God has done for you and your family."

The young man nodded. The pig herders would be angry and perhaps Yeshua's life would be in danger, but he and his father could let everyone know what had really happened.

Thad, his father, and his father's friend knelt at Yeshua's feet. "Please do go. You are in danger here. The Gentiles who own the pig farm will be angry over their loss. We will do anything you want," they said. "Anything at all."

After Yeshua blessed them, they turned and walked sadly down the path. They had wanted to be with the One who had healed them. But soon the joy of what had happened overwhelmed their sorrow and they ran the rest of the way back to the village.

"Look, look," Thad shouted to the first person he saw. "My father is back!"

SAMUEL

amuel sighed as he lifted another beautifully arranged platter of food to his shoulder and carried it into the banqueting room. His father had gotten him a job in the kitchen of Herod's palace. When the Baptist had been arrested and thrown in prison Samuel had feared that he might be arrested too as one of the Baptist's disciples, but as time had passed he felt a little more secure. He worried about the preacher, though.

Part of his job was to take kitchen scraps down to the prison for some of the more well-to-do prisoners. The poor ones relied on food from home or just starved. Father called it a sign of "Herod's guilty conscience" that they were feeding John at all. Herod Antipas had challenged John to make his scathing rebukes to his face. When the Baptist did, the ruler had clapped him in chains and thrown him in the dungeon. However, the Baptist had so many followers and sympathizers that the ruler was afraid to do much more and made sure that John was at least fed. After all, the preacher had not said anything that was not true. People were just shocked that he had the audacity to say it to a ruler like Herod. After the banquet Samuel scraped some of the leftover food onto a plate, covered it, and headed for the dungeon.

The soldiers there knew him by now and swung the door open as he approached. One guard smiled grimly. "They may be leftovers, but John sure eats better than we do."

Samuel laughed. "Yeah, it's pretty rich stuff, and I don't know about him, but it gives me chronic indigestion."

The soldier nodded. "I know what you mean. Strange food in a strange place does that to me too. And the water here. Before we got the aqueducts going, that was enough to make you sick without eating the food."

The boy entered John's cell. "I've brought dinner for you," he said gently.

"I'm not hungry," the Baptist replied, sitting with his back against the wall, his eyes closed.

"Come on, you've got to eat something. Any day now Yeshua of Nazareth is going to take over the government and you'll be out of here. You're going to be all right, and until then you need to keep your health."

"Do you think He ever will?" John asked, his voice sounding tired.

"Of course. That was your whole mission in life—to tell us He was coming."

"What if I was wrong?"

"Wrong?" Samuel asked in surprise. "How could the hundreds of us who left our families and beliefs to follow you—how could that many of us be wrong? No, God sent you. Remember?"

"Some days I can't remember anymore." A tear trickled down his pale cheek. "I was never indoors. Even as a child they had trouble keeping me in. And ever since my father died I roamed the wilderness instead of attending the rabbinical schools. I've never been confined in one place like this. I feel as if I'm dying."

"Please don't feel like that," the boy begged. "Come on, maybe if you just eat something."

The soldier who had been standing guard by the door shook his head. "I don't think eating is going to help him. People who have been outdoors all their lives don't do well in places like this."

"You're no help," Samuel snapped. He turned back to John. "Come on, remember the good times. Good times are coming again."

The preacher just shook his head. Samuel squeezed his hand.

"I'll be back tomorrow. Please eat something before then."

As he left, the soldier patted him on the shoulder. "Don't feel bad, boy. Nothing you do will make a difference. Outdoor people just don't do well in here."

The next day Samuel carried the platter of food across the courtyard and down the many steps and through several gates to the dungeon. He wasn't sure if he looked forward to or dreaded his daily duty. Although he had great respect for the Baptist, still it was hard to see him chained up and becoming thinner and more discouraged every day. Samuel sat down near the edge of the cell as the Baptist picked at his food.

"Do you remember when we asked you about Yeshua of Nazareth?" Samuel began tentatively. The Baptist nodded. "You said that He should increase and you should decrease. And that's exactly what happened." Curious, John glanced at him out of the corner of his eye.

"What I don't understand," the boy continued, "is that all of us following you were so devout. We were really careful to fast on the right days and to spend a lot of time in prayer. The followers of Yeshua don't seem to fast. Every time you turn around, they're going to a different party, including some with social outcasts. They're not careful about the way they wash their hands, the way they keep the law, or anything. Are you sure He's the one you were waiting for?"

John sat with his head in his hands. "I don't know anymore. Maybe you should ask Him."

"What?"

"Yes, why not? Ask Him if He's the one that I was waiting for. And ask Him about the fasting and the praying. I'd like to know." He leaned against the wall and closed his eyes.

"Aren't you going to eat?"

"I've had all I want."

"I'll leave it a little while longer. Maybe if I come back later you'll get your appetite back."

As Samuel headed back toward the kitchens, he decided to ask his father if they could visit Yeshua of Nazareth.

* * *

Samuel's feet fairly flew as he scurried across the courtyard toward the stairwell to the dungeon. He could hardly wait to speak to the Baptist. "Wake up! Wake up! I spoke to your cousin!" the boy said excitedly.

John opened his eyes and tilted his head to one side. "We did what you said," Samuel continued. "We found Yeshua of Nazareth, my father and I, and we asked Him."

Now John was wide awake. "What did He say?"

"At first He didn't say anything, just started healing people. He laid His hands over blind men's eyes and they began to see. There were people there who hadn't walked in years, and all of a sudden they could walk! We saw lepers whose skin was healed and became all pink again. He healed those who couldn't hear too. And He can even raise the dead! Then He told us to come back and tell you what we had seen, and He gave a special blessing for you. He said, 'Blessed is anyone who does not give up his faith because of Me.'"

John had listened intently, then shook his head. "It's too late for me."

Samuel laughed with delight. "No, it's not!" he insisted. "All kinds of people have asked Yeshua to do a sign to prove that He was the Messiah. He's never been willing to do it for anyone, yet when you were discouraged, He did hundreds of them, all with us standing right there waiting. You were important enough for the Messiah to give sign after sign after sign. It's not too late for you! As my father started to leave to get back here, I heard a little bit more. Yeshua asked the crowd just what they thought they had gone out to see when they visited you at the Jordan. Then He said you were the greatest prophet that had ever lived and that no one more important than you has ever been born! He said you were the Elijah who had been foretold by the prophets."

The Baptist leaned forward, tears rolling down his cheeks.

"Oh, there's more, there's more!"

"What more could there be?"

"You know we were upset because His disciples don't fast and pray as much as we do. Well, He turned to the crowd and told them that God had tried hard to speak to them through you, with fasting and prayer and a strict life, and now through Him and His disciples who ate like they did and lived like they did, and that God was doing everything He could to reach every type of person. While some people have accepted Him, the people who were critical of you for your fasting and strict lifestyle are the same ones who attack Him for eating and drinking too much and for being a friend of tax collectors and other sinners."

John nodded. "Yes, I am sure they are the same people."

"Well," Samuel said finally, "all my questions were answered."

John slowly nodded. "Herod can do anything he wants to me now, because I did what I was born to do. Nothing else matters." He leaned against the wall and closed his eyes. Samuel waited for several minutes, and when the Baptist did not say anything further, he quietly left.

SARAH

BETHANY

arah hurried toward the village well. The younger women met there early in the morning to catch up on news and enjoy a few minutes together before the start of another heavy workday.

"Have you heard?" her friend Leah asked.

"Heard what? I just got here."

"Mary's back."

For a moment Sarah just stared at her friend. "She is? She has more courage than I have."

"Yes, they say she returned last night with a whole bunch of men."

"What a surprise," Sarah said bitterly. "But then, what else would you expect from someone like the Magdalene?"

The other women at the well laughed. "I wonder if she's planning to stay," someone asked.

"I certainly hope not," Sarah answered. "We don't need her kind around here."

Leah nodded her agreement. "It's true, but why would she come back?"

"I heard that she was wealthy and doing very well at—what she did in Magdala."

"Maybe she returned to make money here," Sarah suggested.

"In Bethany? Don't be ridiculous," Leah responded. "No rich people come through here, or at least those who do keep going. She must be home for something else. But what?"

Another woman shrugged. "Maybe it has something to do with that big group of men she arrived with. All I know is I am certainly staying away from their house."

Leah nodded. "Me too. It's disgusting. I hope she leaves soon. She must be a great embarrassment to poor Martha and Lazarus. I'm not surprised that Martha hasn't found anyone willing to marry her."

"Well, don't be too hard on her," Sarah replied. "You and I haven't found anyone to marry us either yet."

"I know, but we're only 11," Leah protested.

Sarah laughed. "That's true. I suppose we stand a better chance than Martha does, although she cooks better than either of us."

"She cooks better than anybody," Leah agreed. "Maybe Lazarus doesn't want to let her go."

"Maybe."

Suddenly all the women fell silent as they sensed someone approaching. "I don't believe it," someone said, but the rest quickly shushed her. Martha's younger sister walked through the crowd of staring women, drew water and poured it into her jug, and turned to leave.

"You can stop staring any time now," Mary said. "Yes, it is me. Yes, I'm here. No, I'm not planning to continue my profession here or anywhere else. Yeshua of Nazareth has taken me away from that life and healed me."

"Probably needed it," one of the women harrumphed, "considering your previous line of business and all."

Mary spun around but couldn't spot who had said it. "Yes, I did need it more than you know." Then she trudged back toward her home.

Leah and Sarah stood staring after her. "Yeshua of Nazareth? He's in the group of men she came with!" Leah said in amazement. "He always seemed such a nice man."

Sarah shook her head. "He must not be the real Messiah if He associates with someone like Mary. I'll see you later, Leah. I've got a lot to do." She trudged slowly back to her home, feeling a sense of great disappointment. She had been hoping that Yeshua was the Messiah.

Samuel

HEROD'S PALACE

ervants scurried everywhere, and the kitchen was filled with delicious odors. Every servant in the palace was on duty for the special event. It was Herod's birthday.

There will be lots of leftovers, Samuel thought to himself. *John will have his choice of just about anything here.* He saddened as he remembered how the Baptist grew thinner by the day in his jail cell. Even though Samuel tried to select the best leftovers, John just picked at them and ate very little.

As the evening progressed, the party became wilder. Samuel was delighted that he was able to carry trays of food into the men's great banqueting hall. Dancers from Arabia competed with jugglers from Persia. He saw incredible gifts of gold and exotic animals. Then the music stopped as the last of the jugglers disappeared from the banquet hall. The doors opened and Herodias entered. She wore heavy makeup and not enough clothes in Samuel's opinion. He lowered his eyes. *Our ruler and his wife are an embarrassment,* he thought to himself, *and totally without shame.* A murmur of surprise greeted Herodias since she should have been with the women in their banqueting hall. Herod's notorious wife clapped her hands for everyone's attention. "And now," she said, "we have a special birthday treat for you—my daughter."

As Herodias left, the musicians started playing a sensual song and a young dancer entered the room. Her eyes heavily darkened with the kohl that wealthy women used, she began to dance. Seconds later Samuel felt a hand on his shoulder. It was his father.

"Samuel, get back to the kitchen right now."

"Father, I'm as old as many of the other servers," the boy protested.

His father just shook his head.

Slowly Samuel walked back to the kitchen. He could still hear the music in the background and voices in the great hall. After fixing a platter for the Baptist, he trudged across the courtyard and down the familiar stone steps. The Baptist was looking even more pale and tired tonight. The faint but undulating music had an eerie quality in the underground cell; then it stopped, followed by loud cheering.

"I brought you some of the best stuff," the boy said. "I slipped it out to you early."

The Baptist nodded. "May God bless you for your faithfulness to me."

"I hope He blesses you with freedom really soon," Samuel responded. The Baptist closed his eyes. "Please eat some of it."

Silence filled the cell, broken suddenly by the sounds of footsteps echoing down the corridor. "They must be bringing someone new," Samuel sighed, but the soldiers had no prisoner. They marched straight to John's cell.

"John, son of Zechariah," one soldier said. The Baptist raised his head. The others unhooked the chains that held him in a crouching position against the wall. The Baptist had been there so long he was unable to straighten up fully by himself. They pulled him to a standing position.

"To where?" John asked.

"To the block," a soldier announced. "Your time has come."

"No, no," Samuel protested. "This can't be happening. He's my friend. He's a prophet."

The friendly soldier who often chatted with Samuel seemed not even to notice his presence. He turned on his heel and led the rest, who were supporting the weakened prophet between them.

"No, no, somebody stop them," the boy screamed, then fled up the stairs to find his father. Samuel sobbed and sobbed against his father's chest. His father held him quietly and said nothing.

"Can't we do anything, Father?" he asked.

His father shook his head. "Nothing. Herod is drunk. Herodias had her daughter, Salome, dance for him. Afterward Herod promised her anything she wanted. She ran over to the women's banquet hall and asked her mother what she should request."

"But—but if she could have had anything, why didn't she ask for money or jewels or power or a house?"

"Those may be things she would enjoy, but her mother wanted the head of John the Baptist on a platter. She has hated him ever since she was publicly humiliated when John condemned her sin with Herod. I don't think we will be able to do anything. You must be strong, my son, and you must not speak of your feelings here. It is very dangerous. You have been faithful to the Baptist. Now you must be faithful to what he taught you."

"I can't believe they're really going to kill him."

Suddenly they heard a roar and then silence in the direction of the women's banquet hall. Another servant rushed into the kitchen.

"What's happening?" father asked him.

"They just took the prophet's head in on a platter and presented it to Herodias."

Father looked sick. "Come, Samuel." He and the boy hurried out of the kitchen.

"Where are we going?" the boy inquired as his father led him across the courtyard and down the steps.

"She may have his head, but we're going to get the rest of him." The soldier who had been Samuel's friend stood at the bottom of the steps. When Father and Samuel came rushing down, he nodded to Father, then leaned up against the wall, folded his arms across his chest, and closed his eyes. Father brushed past him into a large room at the end of the cell block. There in a pool of blood rested the prophet's headless body.

"Quickly, Samuel, help me." Taking off his outer cloak, Father rolled the prophet's body onto it. "You get one end, I'll get the other. Hurry, we've only got a few minutes." And gently carrying the prophet's body, the father and son slipped up the stairs and disappeared into the night.

SARAH

BETHANY

aving overslept, Sarah grabbed her water jug and hurried toward the well. Now she would miss most of her friends who, already would have drawn their water and returned to their homes to start the day's bread baking.

Leah was still sitting at the well. "Oh, I'm so glad to see you, Sarah. I was waiting for you. I was about to see if you'd fallen ill."

"No, just overslept."

"I'm glad you're well, for there's something going around."

"Really?" Sarah asked. "I hadn't heard about anything."

"Well, I hear that Lazarus is sick."

"Oh, probably some horrible illness that filthy sister of his brought back from Magdala. You hear all kinds of things about that place."

"They say he's really ill," Leah continued.

"Well, that's what he gets for allowing somebody like that to stay at his house. God must be punishing him for what she's done."

A shadow brushed past her, and she spun around. "I thought if I came this late there wouldn't be anyone else here," Mary said in surprise.

"Well, there won't be now," Sarah snapped. "We're just leaving."

"My brother is very sick," Mary suddenly blurted out.

"That's what we heard," Leah said.

Sarah's face burned as she wondered how much Mary had overheard. Then she tossed her head and said, "Well, maybe you should get your Yeshua of Nazareth to heal him the way He supposedly healed you. Sounds like the whole family could use some healing."

Mary stared at her for several moments, then said, "Yes, I suppose the whole family does. That's a good idea." Turning on her heel, she disappeared down the narrow street.

Two days later I followed Sarah to the well. The girl was late again. It seems to me that she didn't oversleep, but went late on purpose, knowing that Mary avoided the other women. Mary was still filling her family jug when Sarah arrived.

"So, Mary, how is Lazarus doing today?"

The woman turned to her. "He's getting weaker. I didn't realize you cared about Lazarus."

Sarah stared at her feet for a moment as if she could feel the stinging in her conscience, but then she raised her head and said, "It sounds like you really should call your Messiah, this Yeshua, before it's too late."

Mary's eyes filled. "I have."

"And . . . ?"

"I've heard nothing yet. Surely He isn't that far away." The woman shook her head. "I don't understand. But I'm sure He'll be here soon."

Sarah didn't know what else to say, so she turned her back and studied a palm tree until Mary left the well.

I shook my head. These humans, as vulnerable as they all are, are still so cruel to each other. However, such behavior was nothing new to me. I shook my head and continued to follow my charge.

* * *

"Sarah," her mother called. "Sarah, where are you?"

The girl got up from grinding the wheat and went to her mother. "What's the matter?"

"We've just heard that Lazarus died this afternoon. Make some extra bread, and let's prepare for a funeral."

"Does Mary know?"

"Of course," her mother nodded.

A strange expression crossed the daughter's face. "Why are you looking like that?" her mother demanded.

"Nothing. It's just that Mary was going to send for that Yeshua of Nazareth and ask Him to heal Lazarus. She sent for Him three days ago."

"Well, perhaps He was busy," her mother replied.

"I suppose. I guess a little family from Bethany is not as important as the big crowds that He teaches."

Mother stared at her daughter, her head tilted to one side.

"Why are you taking it so hard? I thought you disliked Mary and her family."

The girl shrugged. "I do—I guess. I don't like having people like her in our village."

Mother studied her for a minute. "You know, Mary has changed. She doesn't do that anymore. It seems that after she met Yeshua she left all of that behind her. Since then she has been living a respectable life in her family home. Why is that a problem to you?"

"Well, we all know what she is."

Her mother sighed. "Sometimes people do things like that because they've been badly hurt when they were younger. We would probably be better off if we were to treat such people with kindness. You never know when you might need someone to be kind to you. "And," she said, "perhaps but for someone else's kindness, some of the people you love could be in the same position as Mary."

"Nobody in my family. I would just die of shame."

"I see," Mother said, then turned and walked away.

"Now, what's the matter with her?" Sarah wondered out loud.

I shook my head. This young one had a lot to learn. I just wished she could do it without hurting other people so much.

* * *

It had been three days since the funeral. Sarah had not seen Mary at the well again. When she returned to the house with water Mother was stacking extra bread on a plate in a basket and pulling her shawl around her shoulders. "Come with me, Sarah; we're going to visit Mary and Martha."

"I—I just got back with the water," the girl protested. "I have some chores to do."

Mother stopped and gave her a long look, then commanded, "Come with me."

Obediently Sarah turned and followed her mother. "Bring that jar," Mother said. "We'll get them some extra water at the well too. They will probably be needing it."

Then they walked in silence to the house. Sarah had not been inside their home before. She stepped into the courtyard and looked around. It was neat and clean and reminded her of her own home. Martha came out to meet them.

"Oh, thank you so much. And thank you for baking. I just haven't had the time or the energy these past few days."

"I know," Mother said. "That's why we brought some. And Sarah has drawn some water for you."

The girl set the jug down beside the kitchen area, and Martha laid a clean linen cloth over the mouth of it to keep stray flies from drowning.

"How is Mary?" Mother asked.

"She has spent most of the time asleep the past few days. Because she and Lazarus were always very close, she's taking it extra hard."

"Have you heard anything from Yeshua of Nazareth?"

Martha shook her head. "No. But I wish He would come back soon. It would be comforting to Mary. She needs to get up and start doing some normal things that will help her get through this."

Mother nodded. "Sarah and I will assist you with the chores that Mary would usually do. Sometimes rest is the best thing for a broken heart—at least for a few days."

"Here, Sarah," Mother directed, "take the broom and sweep the courtyard. Everything should be neat and clean when Yeshua and His friends return."

Silently Sarah took the broom and headed for a corner of the courtyard. It almost sounded as if Mother was looking forward to Yeshua's return as much as Mary. After the girl finished sweeping the courtyard she found Mother hugging Martha.

"Oh, thank you," the woman said, stepping away from Mother. "If I can walk for a while maybe I will feel better."

"Take as long as you want," Mother responded. "Sarah and I will stay here in case Mary needs anything."

"Thank you," Martha repeated, heading for the doorway.

It startled Sarah a little later when Martha burst into the courtyard and walked hurriedly through the house toward Mary's sleeping quarters.

"Did you have a good walk?" the girl asked politely.

Martha nodded as she brushed past her. Seconds later Mary emerged from the sleeping chamber she and Martha shared, her hair disheveled and her eyes red and puffy. She pulled her outer garment on, fastening the tie at the waist as she went.

"Where are you going?" Sarah asked. Neither of them answered her, so she followed them. Mother also went with them.

"Maybe they're going back to the grave to weep some more," Sarah suggested to her mother. "We could go wail with them."

"Maybe," Mother muttered, hurrying to catch up. Sarah shrugged and kept walking. Wherever they were heading, it would be better than sitting around the house looking for chores to do. As they reached the edge of town, Sarah saw a group of travelers. Mary broke into a run.

"Yeshua," she shouted, "Yeshua." She ran and threw herself at His feet, sobbing. Martha started crying too. To Sarah's amazement, Yeshua's own eyes filled with tears.

"Where have you buried him?" He asked. The women led Him to the family tomb.

"In there," they said. By now tears poured down Yeshua's face.

Sarah couldn't believe it. He was crying with them. Then to her great surprise, He commanded, "Roll the stone back."

Sarah shuddered. "But Master," Martha protested, "he's been dead for four days now and will stink terribly. You really don't want to do this."

"Yes, I do," He continued. "Roll the stone away."

The men who were with Him tugged at the stone blocking the

tomb entrance. What was Yeshua going to do? Sarah had heard that He could do miracles and heal blind people. Rumors even claimed that He had brought a dead boy back to life, but surely no one actually believed that.

Yeshua glanced toward heaven and said, "Father, I thank You that You have heard Me. You always hear Me, but today My friends who are with Me will see it too and believe that You sent Me."

Sarah felt as if her hair were standing on end. Was He really talking to God that way, as though He was a family member?

Suddenly Yeshua shouted, "Lazarus, come out of there." Everyone stared as they heard a shuffling noise in the cave. Then Lazarus, still wrapped from head to toe in the graveclothes they had wound around him, came shuffling toward the tomb entrance.

"Well," Yeshua said, "untangle him; let him loose."

Instantly they rushed forward. After they unwound Lazarus someone flung a cloak around him. Everyone was laughing and shouting and talking all at once. Sarah just stood and shivered. *Could it be? Could He have actually raised Lazarus from the dead? Obviously He had. Could He really be the Messiah? If He was not, He would be a powerful enemy.* She glanced around. Many others in the crowd that had gathered also stood there silently. She wondered if they too had trouble believing in this Teacher from Nazareth. When she searched for Yeshua again, He had disappeared.

While spirits don't weep the way humans do, my eyes would have filled with tears if they could have. What more could Yeshua do that would startle these people out of their doubt? What else could He do to prove He was the Son of God? I shook my head. Nothing. The Creator had made these creatures with the power of choice. They could believe Him or not, and unless He took away that power to choose, there was nothing He or I could do about it. A great sadness filled me as I stood watching the celebrating crowd, for my young charge was not one of them.

DAVID

LEPER COLONY

ecording David's life and his choices had been painful. Terrible things had happened to him, but instead of drawing him closer to the Comforter of Israel, each tragedy had made him harder and more bitter. Losing his beautiful young wife in childbirth seemed to be the last straw that any man could bear, and then to be diagnosed as a leper on top of it was crushing.

I had watched him leave the Temple on that fateful day, carrying his toddler, who, though glowing with health, would soon be rotting like all the other lepers if taken to the colony. Unfortunately, David had no other choice. Now I quivered with excitement, knowing the surprise that waited for him. The closer he came to the leper colony outside the city, the more depressed he became and the slower his footsteps. The little one he carried was sound asleep, his curly auburn hair like his father's.

The leper colony was a polite word for the garbage dump where the lepers had found some caves to live in. They were able to paw through the garbage and sometimes find food, though the lucky ones had family bring food and leave it for them. As David approached, the other lepers left their caves and stared at him and his child.

"Why did you bring a child here?" asked an older man with a huge oozing sore where his nose used to be.

David tried not to stare at him. "I had no choice. Do you think I would bring my son into a place like this on purpose?"

"You are a leper?"

Nodding, David pulled back the neckline of his robe and rolled up his sleeve to show them the white scaly patches. "Yes, but the boy is not."

"He soon will be," grunted an old man.

Another man stepped forward, though his head was covered with a ragged brown hood and David couldn't see his face clearly. "Come," he said. "We have room in my cave."

The cave smelled bad, yet David was thankful for the hospitality.

"Your name?" asked the hooded man.

"David."

"Ah. You remind me so of someone I once knew. What town are you from?"

"I was born in Bethlehem," David answered, "but I haven't lived there for years."

"Why?"

Staring at the wall beyond the man's head, David replied, "I don't really want to talk about it."

The old man grunted. "Who was your mother?"

The younger leper faced him. "For an outcast, you ask a lot of questions."

"I've been gone a long time," the old man said slowly. "I hunger for news of home. I too was from Bethlehem."

The younger man's forehead wrinkled in puzzlement. "If you were from Bethlehem, what are you doing with these lepers? Why aren't you with those outside Bethlehem?"

"Ah, now *you* ask a lot of questions. Do you remember the name of your mother?"

David stared. "Why are you asking me this? Who are you?"

The old man drew his hood back so David could see him. His first response was to recoil in disgust. The man's face had been so eaten away by the disease that he no longer looked human. But that hair—curly red hair—was just like his.

"Who are you?" David demanded.

The disfigured leper now wept openly. "My son," he said. "My son. You grew up into a handsome man. How could you have this disease too? What horrible trick fate has played on us."

"Yes," David spat, "fate or God. Why did you leave us? You did leave us."

The old man nodded. "Your mother begged me not to leave, but as a leper in Bethlehem, I would have been chased out of the town once people found out. And with her as a widow, my property would have reverted to my family, and your mother to my brother. If I just disappeared it allowed some time. Your mother was not disgraced by a divorce, and everyone would wait, for a time at least, in case I came back. It was the best thing I could do for my family. I was desperate."

Filled with rage, David stood and punched the cave wall with his free arm. His little son woke up and started to cry. "It's OK, it's OK," David soothed him. "Father's not angry at you." He glanced up at the disfigured leper. "I guess I'm not even angry at you. I never knew."

"I know," the old man choked out, "but what could I have told you?"

"Well, now there are three generations of us here rotting in this stinking pit. The God of Israel must really hate sons of Bethlehem with red hair."

His father nodded as his grandson looked up at him with wide eyes.

I shook my head. David had finally found his father, and yet he still cursed the Most High. Surely this human was bitter to the core. Was there anything redeemable in him at all? I wondered.

* * *

It had only been a few weeks, yet already David and his little one looked as filthy and tattered as the rest of the leprous beggars. Every day he checked the toddler for white patches on his dirty little body, but so far all he noted was that both he and the child were rapidly losing weight.

"Son, there's a crowd coming along the road here," his father called. "Come out of the cave."

"Why? I'm busy."

"Yeah, staring off into the darkness. Quit feeling sorry for yourself. It's Yeshua of Nazareth. We've heard wonderful things about Him."

"Yeah, I bet you have. I've heard more than I want to hear about Him."

"Oh, come on. I hear He can heal leprosy."

David rolled his eyes. "And why would He want to do that, even if He could? Face it. The God of Israel hates us. And if this Yeshua really is the Messiah, He'll probably hate us too."

The old man glared at him. "What do you have to lose? You've already lost everything else. Are you afraid of giving up this stinking cave? Are you afraid of losing life as a leper, because you're looking forward someday to having a face like mine, a fate like mine?"

David stared at his father's feet and noticed for the first time that many toes were missing. *No wonder he limps,* he thought.

"May you and your pride rot right here in Gehenna," his father shouted. "But I am going to see this Yeshua. What do I have to lose? If all else fails, I'll be back, but if He is the Messiah, I won't be. I've prayed for you all these years and I love you, my son, but not enough to stay here."

Just then little Jonathan, David's son, ran into the cave and grabbed his father's hand. "Come on, Father," he begged. "Let's go with Grandfather! Come on."

David got to his feet and, between his father and his little redheaded son, headed for the road, squinting at the brightness of the sunlight. As they neared the edge of the crowd, the lepers automatically began shouting, "Unclean, unclean."

Little Jonathan laughed at the crowd's reaction. "It's like the parting of the Red Sea, Father. Look at those people get out of the way."

His grandfather would have laughed if he hadn't been so ashamed. But instead he called, "Yeshua, Son of David, the first David, have mercy on us!"

"Yes," the child echoed, "have mercy on us."

Suddenly the last of the people moved to the side and they stood before Yeshua of Nazareth. David felt as if His piercing eyes could see right into his soul. He returned the gaze for a few moments and then whispered, "Have mercy on me, too, Yeshua of Nazareth," and dropped to his knees. Would He heal them? Would He bless them, or would He just send them away?

"Go," Yeshua said in a loud voice. David's heart sank until he heard the rest of the instruction. "Go show yourselves to the priests."

David looked down at his body, pulling his sleeve up. He peeked inside his tattered robe. The white patches were gone! He turned to his father. The open draining sores that had once been the beggar's face had vanished. Instead he was an impressive-looking man, the father David dimly remembered from his childhood.

Scooping little Jonathan up with one arm, he hugged his father with the other. "Look at us!" he shouted. "Look at us!" They turned to the other lepers. The 10 of them danced in a circle. "Look at us, we're whole! Let's go to the Temple and show that priest a thing or two. He'll have to declare us clean now."

Grandfather scooped up little Jonathan and started to run with the rest of the lepers back toward the city. David followed for several yards, then stopped. "Come on," shouted his father.

"I'll catch up with you." David then turned and walked slowly back through the crowd. Falling on his knees before Yeshua, he burst into tears. "Thank You," he said. "Thank You."

Yeshua of Nazareth looked at the healed man. "There were 10," He commented.

Slowly David bowed his head in acknowledgment. "Gratitude

does not always come easily for those of us who have had hard times," he said haltingly. Yeshua nodded.

"You have healed me, and You've healed my life. I have a father and a son. I have a life worth living."

The Teacher smiled. "Go show yourself to the priest. You're not officially healed till you do that."

It was the law. "The priests are important," David said, "but even more important is my Messiah."

ELIHU BEN MALCHUS

JERICHO

eshua of Nazareth is coming," a youngster shouted as he ran down the street. Elihu turned to his father. "May I go?" he asked. "I'd like to see him." The boy had heard of the Teacher, but had not had a chance to listen to Him in the throng-filled Temple and teaming city of Jerusalem. Now his family was visiting relatives in Jericho, and the Galilean was also in town. Here at last was his chance to hear Him.

Malchus frowned. "You may go, but don't get involved with that group. He's a troublemaker."

"That's what I've heard," Elihu said. "But I just want to see Him."

His father nodded. "Yes, but keep your distance and don't become a disciple of His."

Elihu laughed. "You raised me better than that, Father."

"I hope so. As a servant of a high priest, I've tried to give you nothing but the best education, so mind you, don't forget it all around this preacher. I hear He is almost as charismatic as that John fellow who baptized down by the river before Herod had his head chopped off."

"I'll be careful, Father," he said, and then ran down the street.

The crowd was huge, and people shoved against each other. Elihu tried to wiggle his way through to the front, but no one would let anyone else through. Then the boy tripped, and for a moment terror gripped him. The crowd kept right on pushing and stepping on him. "Help me, help me," he screamed, but no one seemed to hear. Finally he clawed at a man's robe and used it to pull himself up. *No one is worth getting trampled to death to see,* he thought to himself as he pushed his way over to the side.

The crowd was still moving in his direction. He looked quickly to the left and right. Not far away was a sycamore fig tree that leaned its branches out over the road. Dusting himself off, Elihu sprinted toward the tree and swung up onto a low overhanging branch. Suddenly he started as he realized he was not alone. He caught his breath sharply. What should he do? He was sharing a tree with the most hated man in town: Zacchaeus, the tax collector. Everyone knew that tax collectors were collaborators with the Romans. But if that wasn't enough, Zacchaeus was known for charging double and blackmailing people who owed taxes just to line his own pockets.

The tax collector nodded in greeting to him. Elihu looked the other way as he had been taught. *What a creepy little man,* he thought. *Perhaps God has punished him for his sins by not allowing him to grow very tall.* Then he chuckled to himself. Of course, that was probably why Zacchaeus was in the tree—for the same reason as Elihu. He couldn't see over the crowd either. They both sat in silence on the branch in anticipation, waiting for Yeshua of Nazareth to pass below so that they could get a good look at Him.

Sure enough, the crowd went by directly under the tree. Zacchaeus seemed to be trying to make himself smaller and hide among the dusty leaves as he peered at the famous Teacher. Suddenly the crowd stopped. Yeshua looked straight up into the tree right at the tax collector. "Zacchaeus," He said. "Come down. I'm on My way to your house for dinner."

Elihu's jaw dropped, as did that of Zacchaeus. The boy couldn't believe it. A renowned Teacher who traveled all over the country was going to have dinner with a national traitor?

Quickly Elihu climbed to another branch as Zacchaeus scrambled down out of the tree. The little man joined Yeshua, and the crowd moved on. For a long time Elihu sat in his leafy perch thinking. *Why would the Rabbi have dinner with the tax collector? Did He not know the little man's profession? Or more amazing yet, if He did, was He trying to show the rest of the crowd that He accepted Zacchaeus anyway?*

The boy shook his head in puzzlement. Yeshua seemed a likable man. Certainly the crowds flocked to Him. What was it about Him? Again Elihu shook his head. He wasn't sure, but he had to get home before supper, or Father would be worried.

SARAH

he whole town buzzed with excitement. Their most important citizen, Simon the Pharisee, was planning a feast. It was going to be a huge party, and he had hired several local young people to serve the guests. Sarah was one of them. Until two weeks ago she would have been delighted with the prospect of serving important guests in the fanciest house in town. Yet now it tied her stomach in knots at just the idea of going there.

As she stood in the kitchen area waiting with the others for her serving instructions her mind kept going back to her friend, Leah, sobbing in her arms. "No one will ever marry me now," the girl cried. "I'm a disgrace to my family. I don't know what to do."

Sarah had tried to comfort her the best she could, but she hadn't known what to do either. She knew that according to the law of Moses the person who did this to her friend should either take her to wife or pay a heavy fine, but he was Simon the Pharisee, so likely nothing would happen except that Leah was in disgrace. Sure enough, Leah's family had been tight-lipped about the whole thing, but the next day Leah was gone. When Sarah had asked about her, her mother had just said, "She has gone to stay with her aunt."

Sarah grieved over the loss of her friend and hated Simon for it. And now she was in his house to serve at his feast. She had told her father that she didn't want to, but he merely said, "It is an honor and you will go," so she did.

As she carried the first tray of food into the banquet room, she almost dropped it in surprise. There at the head of the table near Simon was his honored guest—Yeshua. The Teacher looked right at her and smiled, filling her with confusion. Who was this man? Lazarus was a guest at the table too. She couldn't forget the day that Yeshua had resurrected Lazarus. If Yeshua had raised him from the dead minutes after his death, some might have questioned whether Lazarus had really died, but the man had been dead and buried for days.

Her mind was a jumble of confusion the whole evening as she moved mechanically back and forth from the cooking area to the banquet chamber. Her back ached, but she still had more trays to carry. She lifted another to her shoulder and entered the dining area when something startled her. It was a beautiful and familiar aroma. What was it? As she moved toward the table she suddenly recognized it as perfume—the kind used to embalm bodies. She remembered it now from Lazarus' funeral. It was the same scent, except much stronger.

Suddenly she figured out where it was coming from. Mary, Lazarus' sister, had slipped into the room and poured it over Yeshua's feet. Then realizing she had no towel with her, she wiped it with her long hair. Sarah was horrified. Letting her hair down in public was an admission to the whole crowd what type of woman Mary was, for no respectable woman would do such a thing—but then Yeshua must know that if He had healed her.

Sarah glanced at Simon. As she placed the food from the tray on the table she heard him whispering to another guest. "If He knew what kind of woman she was, He wouldn't let her touch His feet."

Mary looked at Yeshua. He had heard it too. Then Mary's eyes met Simon's. Suddenly Sarah froze. The look on Mary's face was the same as that on Leah's face when she had stumbled into Sarah's house sobbing and bleeding. Could it be? Had Mary become the kind of woman she was because of what Simon had done to *her* when she was younger?

"Simon, I have a question for you," Yeshua said, breaking the tense silence.

Snatching her tray back, Sarah stumbled from the room, Mary following quietly behind her, her sleeve hiding her face. Sarah faced her. "Mary, I'm so sorry." She wrapped her arms around the woman and they both began to sob. "I'm so sorry I was mean to you. I didn't know; I never knew. I didn't understand."

"Yeshua has forgiven me for everything," Mary managed to say between sobs, "and He's healed me. It's just that I don't understand why He came to Simon's house. He healed Simon of leprosy. Did you know that?"

Sarah shook her head.

"It was in the early stages, but Yeshua healed him. I don't understand why, but I'll always love Him for bringing me away from that terrible life."

"The perfume," Sarah suddenly realized. "That was your savings."

Mary nodded. "The money I made in Magdala—I needed to invest it in something or hide it in some way so it wouldn't be stolen from me, so I bought this alabaster box and this expensive perfume. But I can't think of anyone I would have rather used it for."

The two women slipped out of the kitchen and sat in the moonlight, comforting each other. I watched them, and was sorry they didn't hear what Yeshua said to the Pharisee.

"Simon," He had said, "if two servants owed a rich man money—one of them a small amount and the other a great amount—and he forgave them both, which one would love him more?"

"I suppose the one whom he forgave more," Simon reluctantly acknowledged, his eyes meeting Yeshua's and then dropping to the floor. And he got the point. I could tell from way over here where I stood with the weeping women. Without exposing his sin to any of the other guests, Yeshua let Simon know that He knew. How kind He was, how patient with fragile human egos. I was amazed.

David

avid strode confidently into the village with his young son on his shoulders and his father beside him. Life was good. They had returned to Bethlehem and repaired the broken-down home that Father had abandoned so many years before. The roof had fallen in with the rains, but the stonework was as sound as it had ever been. To David's amazement, the gold coins—given to him so many years ago by the wealthy men who came to honor the Baby—still remained hidden under the loose stones in the hearth. That was just enough for them to start their life again. Now it was almost time for Passover, and they were able to afford to make the trip to Jerusalem. They even had enough extra money to buy a donkey. One of the travelers on the road had told David about a young colt in the village of Bethphage.

"Just think," he said to little Jonathan on his shoulders, "if we buy a little donkey for you, you won't have to ride on my shoulders all the way home."

"Or walk," Grandfather added.

Jonathan giggled. The family with the colt for sale was not difficult to find. They struck a deal, and money changed hands.

"Daddy, I'm hungry," the child complained.

"Well, I am too," his grandfather replied. "Perhaps we can buy some food here in this town and have some lunch before we finish our journey. Then we need to get to Jerusalem and rent space to stay for Passover."

David nodded. "Yes, I want to get a room before the crowds arrive, but let's find some lunch first."

They tied the donkey to a little post next to a woman selling bread and curds of cheese. Just then they noticed a large group of men approaching. One of them hurried ahead and came straight to David and his family. David recognized him as one of Yeshua's disciples.

"The Lord has need of your colt," he told the young man. David and his father broke into smiles as he untied the colt and handed her reins to the man. She had never been ridden before, and David and his father knew that an ancient tradition said that the Messiah would arrive on a colt.

"Look at this," David said to his father as the disciple led the colt hurriedly back to the group. "We're here just at the right time. We're going to see the Messiah crowned King."

"The King, the King!" little Jonathan repeated, clapping his hands. "I want to see the King. When can I ride the donkey?"

"The King is going to ride our donkey," his father replied. Pulling out a knife, he whacked off some branches from a low growing palm next to the road. "Here's a little one for you, my son. We're going to a coronation!"

The word spread and soon other travelers and villagers filled the road, waving branches and shouting, "Hosanna, hosanna!" ("O save, O save"). And there in the center rode the Messiah on David's new colt.

What an honor, David thought as he shouted with the rest of the crowd, *"Blessed is He who comes in the name of the Lord."*

* * *

"David," Grandfather said several days later, "somehow we have this huge room for just the three of us."

His son laughed. "Yes, it is large, but it's what was available."

"When I go to the Temple today," Grandfather continued, "if I run across any of the other lepers whom Yeshua healed along with us, I think I'll bring them back to celebrate the Passover with us. We have so much room."

"That's a good idea. While you buy the lamb to take to the Temple, I will fetch water and buy unleavened bread and bitter herbs in the market so that we will have everything ready for the evening meal."

"Excellent," Grandfather said. "I'll take young Jonathan with me. It will be hard for you to balance a water jug along with the other purchases while keeping track of him."

"Are we going to see Yeshua at the Temple?" Jonathan asked.

"I don't know," Grandfather answered. "He goes there quite often and teaches during the daytime."

"We're going to see Yeshua!" the boy shouted.

"He might not be there," David cautioned. "I heard He caused a real incident yesterday. He threw out the money changers again and several of the priests who were cheating the people."

Grandfather laughed. "Good for Him. There are good priests, but too many of them are just dishonest leeches feeding off people who bring what little they have to God."

David nodded. "Yes, and if Yeshua of Nazareth is the Messiah, He has every right to clean out His house."

They all nodded. Jonathan clapped his hands. "Yeshua rode my donkey. Can we give Yeshua another ride on my donkey?"

"Not today," Grandfather said, picking him up. "Passover is coming, and you're going to learn all about that. Come on, little one."

The older man and the little boy left hand in hand to purchase a lamb while David picked up a large water jug and headed down the steps toward the well in the Kidron Valley. They were fortunate to have been able to rent the whole upper room of a house, and he hoped his father would find some friends to share it with.

It didn't take long for David to get the things he needed in the market and, balancing the full water jug, he headed back toward their rented room. On the way two men approached him. Again they looked familiar. "The Master says that His time has come and He wants to celebrate the Passover at your place with His disciples," one of them told him.

David broke into a huge smile. Strange how he had run into Yeshua's disciples still another time. "It is prepared. Come, I'll show you where I am staying. How did you pick me?" David asked the taller of the two men.

"The Master told us to look for a man carrying water," he replied, "and by the way, my name is Peter."

"Good to meet you, Peter." David laughed. "I guess it is unusual to see a man carrying water. After all, it is women's work. It's just that in our family we have no women right now. I think all men should be widowed for a short period of time before they get married. It would make them appreciate their women a whole lot more."

Peter and the other disciple laughed. "Yes, but it's hard to be widowed if you weren't married first."

As they entered the rented room, Peter and John looked around. "This will be great," they said.

"I have food for the supper," David explained, "and my father is on the way back from buying a lamb. We will get it roasting, and everything will be ready for tonight."

"Excellent, excellent," they said. "We will join you later."

The Passover supper was wonderful. David and his father enjoyed having company to share the dinner with and they fit in well, for Yeshua and His disciples were also without any wives that week, although David knew some of them were married.

When the Passover dinner ended, the disciple named Judas slipped out apparently to take care of some business while Yeshua and His other disciples sat chatting. David scooped up his son and went to the far end of the room and unrolled his sleeping mat. There he sat leaning against the wall, snuggling and gently rocking the child and humming a little song. Ever since his wife had died, David had done this every night. It was their bedtime ritual.

He heard snatches of the conversation between Yeshua and His disciples at the other end of the room. It was a little confusing to him without hearing the whole thing. It almost sounded as if the Teacher was planning to leave or die or something. David would have to ask Him about it later. His son's curly little head had fallen on David's chest. Although the child was asleep, David continued to hold him and rested his own head against the wall with his eyes closed.

"I'm giving you a new commandment," he heard Yeshua say to His disciples. "I want you to love each other the way that I have loved you. And I want you to treat each other the way that I have treated you. This is how other people will know that you're My disciple. Not by the clothes you wear, the things you eat, or the way you quote scripture, but by the way you treat other people."

The disciples nodded. Then Yeshua took some of the unleavened bread. "I want to make a new covenant with you." Breaking the bread, He passed it to each of them and said, "This is My body. I'm giving it for you."

The disciples stared at Him wide-eyed. David opened his eyes too. Then Yeshua picked up the cup of wine and passed it to them, saying, "Drink all of it. This is My blood which is shed for you." The disciples soberly passed it around, each one taking a sip. *Why are they doing that?* David wondered. He didn't understand.

Then Yeshua continued, "I will not drink any more wine until the day I come and take you home. I want you to do this in memory of Me. Every time you drink the juice of the grape and eat the unleavened bread, you'll remember Me and what I've done for you and look forward to going home with Me."

I wonder where He's going, David thought sleepily.

Elihu ben Malchus

lihu could sense the tension in the air. Exciting things were happening. His father had been running back and forth all over town with messages. Whatever was going on he wanted to be in on it. That evening his family had the Passover supper as they did every year. But as soon as they finished, his father jumped up and threw on his cloak.

"Father, where are you going?" he asked.

"I have business to attend to."

"Let me come."

Malchus looked at his son for several moments, thinking it over. "Yes," he said. "There are some important things happening tonight and you should come. These are things you will hear a lot about, perhaps, and you need to know what is happening."

His mother said, "But Malchus . . ."

"Hush. He's not a little boy anymore. Come on, son."

"Where are we going?"

"Well, first of all we're going to the high priest's house to meet with some others, and then we're going to capture Yeshua of Nazareth."

The boy's eyes widened. "You are?"

"He's made many enemies of important people that He shouldn't have crossed," his father continued. "It's much too dangerous to arrest him in the Temple, where he talks to the people all of the time, but he has a habit of going to the cave with the olive press over on the hillside there—Gethsemane. Often he sleeps and prays there in the evenings. We're going to catch him there."

"He hasn't done anything really bad, has he?" Elihu asked.

Malchus grimaced. "Offending the high priest and calling his servants who work in the Temple courtyard a bunch of thieves is really bad."

"Oh." The boy had many mixed feelings. Yeshua of Nazareth didn't seem to be a bad person, yet all of his father's friends hated him. Later, leaving the high priest's house, they set out for Gethsemane. Father accompanied the Temple police along with a man named Judas Iscariot. He looked familiar.

"Father," he whispered. "Isn't Judas one of Yeshua's disciples?"

His father nodded.

"Well, then, why is he with us? Won't he warn Yeshua to get away?"

Malchus laughed. "No, he's going to take us to him."

The boy felt sick. It was bad enough to have a bunch of important people hate you, but to have one of your best friends betray you like that—He felt sorry for Yeshua.

"Now, quiet everyone," Father said as they approached Gethsemane.

"There He is," Judas whispered. Then he walked up to Yeshua and kissed Him on the cheek. "Greetings, Master."

"Get him," Malchus shouted, and the Temple police rushed forward. Suddenly there was a blinding flash of light. Elihu wasn't sure what had happened.

Even though the angel guardians were not going to be able to prevent the death the Son of God must face, they did want the mob to know exactly whom they were dealing with, and so they rushed between Yeshua and the crowd. Elihu and everyone around him instantly fell to the ground. After a moment of silence they began stumbling back to their feet while they tried to recover their dignity.

"Whom are you looking for?" Yeshua asked calmly.

"We're looking for Yeshua of Nazareth," Father said.

"I am He," the Teacher replied. "You are really brave men, sneaking out here in the dark with all your swords and sticks to capture Me. I've been sitting in the Temple talking every single day without weapons or anything and you didn't do a thing. Slipping around in the dark is more your style."

Elihu looked up as a movement caught the corner of his eye. One of the disciples had pulled a sword from under his cloak and, yelling at the top of his voice, rushed directly toward his father. "Father!" Elihu shouted, then covered his face. Malchus ducked and instead of being decapitated, had his ear cleanly sliced off. Blood spurted from the side of his head. The boy flung his arms around his father as the blood poured down and soaked his cloak too.

"Father, are you all right?" he asked.

Calmly Yeshua of Nazareth leaned over and picked up the ear lying in the dirt. Then reaching up to Malchus' face, He reattached the ear. The bleeding stopped. Suddenly everyone held up their torches so they could get a better look. The ear stayed, and it looked healthy. Elihu clung to his father as Malchus stood speechless with his arms about his son, staring at Yeshua of Nazareth.

The Teacher turned to Peter, who, breathing heavily, still gripped his dripping sword. "Put your sword away, Peter. This is what My Father has planned. I need to do it."

The disciple turned and disappeared into the night. The crowd surged forward and led Yeshua away. Elihu and Malchus still clung to each other. They would never be the same again.

Aпτoпiα

"etronius, where are we going to be staying in Jerusalem?" Antonia asked.

"At the Antonia fortress," the old servant replied. "It's not every centurion's daughter that has a fortress named after her."

The girl laughed with delight. "Very funny, Petronius. They named it that long before I was born."

"See, they were expecting you."

"Seriously," the girl continued, "where are we going to stay? I know Father will bunk in the fortress with his men because they all have to be in Jerusalem during Passover."

"Yes, whenever all the pilgrims gather in Jerusalem, all the Romans need to be there too so that we can preserve a little order and dignity and prevent any uprisings. These Hebrew holidays make Pilate extremely nervous."

"That's understandable, considering all of the uprisings they've had," Antonia observed.

Petronius sighed. "I certainly hope nothing like that happens while we're here."

The girl shuddered. She had seen enough horrible things as it was. Roman punishments were swift and cruel, and the girl tried not to think about them when she encountered such things. After all, Rome had to keep order somehow.

"You will be staying in the Antonia fortress," said Petronius, "but not in the barracks, like your father and me. The governor's wife has invited you to stay with her."

"Pilate's wife?" she asked in disbelief.

"Yes. Why not? You have no mother, she has no children, and you would enjoy each other's company. Roman women in this part of the world can get pretty lonely."

"That's true," she said slowly. "Maybe this will be a good visit after all."

* * *

Father and his men had gone ahead to the barracks, but Petronius and Antonia encountered a huge crowd gathering in an open area that served as a place of justice and judgment. The girl slipped her hand into Petronius' large calloused one. Large crowds of Judeans made her nervous. This one seemed to be dragging some man around, perhaps a criminal of some sort.

"Come on," Petronius urged, glancing in the mob's direction. "We can enter over here. It's best that we don't get mixed up with this."

Antonia looked back over her shoulder. Pilate was coming out on a balcony and talking with what appeared to be the crowd's leaders. She shuddered, suddenly glad that she could stay in the residential part of the fortress away from the ugly things that might happen outside.

A servant ushered Petronius and Antonia into the residence chambers. "The governor's wife will be with you in just a moment," he said.

Claudia, Pilate's wife, a regal-looking woman dressed in the finest imported eastern silks and with her hair and makeup perfectly done, soon entered the reception chamber. But the woman seemed extremely upset about something as she nervously adjusted her garments.

"Welcome, child," she said. "I am delighted that you're here to spend the week with us. Petronius, you may leave us; we'll be fine."

"Is there anything I can help with before I leave?"

She looked at him for a moment, as if trying to decide whether to tell him something or not. Then, taking a breath, she said, "I hear the crowd out there has returned. Do they have that man with them?"

Petronius studied her for a moment. "They did have what appeared to be some kind of prisoner."

"Oh." The woman winced. "My husband was hoping that by sending him to Herod he would get out of having to deal with this. This is terrible."

"Who is he, may I ask?" Petronius said.

"His name is Yeshua of Nazareth."

"Yeshua," Antonia gasped. "I know Him."

"You do?" Claudia asked incredulously. "Tell me, where have you met Him, and what do you know about Him?"

The girl told her of Petronius' illness and how Yeshua had just spoken the word and healed the servant. She also related how her Hebrew friend Deborah had become so ill that her father, Jairus, had gone to Yeshua to ask for help, and that Deborah had died before Jairus was able to make it back with the Teacher.

"Oh, that's so sad," Claudia commented.

"Actually, it wasn't," Antonia said excitedly. "Yeshua came back and dismissed the mourners and told them she was just sleeping. They all laughed at Him. With just Jairus and his wife and His disciples He went into the house and left the mourners outside. Taking Deborah by the hand, He raised her up and she opened her eyes. Then they fed her lunch and she was just fine."

Claudia seemed more agitated than ever. "You see, I knew it. I knew it."

"You knew what?" Antonia asked.

"The Judeans are having their own Messiah executed."

The girl caught her breath. "Father said I wasn't ever supposed to call Him that where anyone could hear it."

Claudia looked at her and nodded. "And so you shouldn't. It is dangerous here in Jerusalem, but you and I and Petronius know who this Man is."

Suddenly Antonia realized with a terrible pain in her chest why Pilate's wife was so upset. "Was that the person they were pushing around in the courtyard—was that Yeshua?" she stammered.

Her host reluctantly nodded.

"Oh," she said in a choked little voice. "I didn't even recognize Him. They have done terrible things to Him."

"I'm sure they have," Claudia commented.

"He had blood all over Him," Antonia continued. "It looked as if someone had made a crown out of great big briars and pushed it down on His head. He had bruises all over Him, and He was bleeding everywhere."

"Yes, yes," Claudia interrupted. "We have to do something about this."

"But what?" Antonia said. "I don't even know where to find my father."

"I'm not sure your father can do anything about this, but my husband can. The Judeans cannot execute anyone without Roman permission. I must get a message to him right away before they do any more injustice to this good Man. It may be that the Judeans reject their Messiah, but those of us who know who He is must do everything we can to save His life."

She summoned a servant. "I must send a message to Pilate right away. I have had the most terrible nightmares all night about this Man."

"Terrible nightmares?" Antonia looked puzzled. "He's such a good Man; what could have given you nightmares?"

"I'm sure He is a good Man. I dreamed that I awakened and was brought out of the ground as if I had been dead and buried. Everything around me was different. I did not recognize where I was. I saw many buildings that did not look like any that I know. Earthquake after earthquake was ripping the ground apart. Fires raged everywhere, and water flooded some of the streets. Everyone was rushing about, screaming in fear. The light was so bright it hurt my eyes. Yeshua of Nazareth was sitting on something in the clouds above the city with thousands and thousands of shining warriors about Him in the sky. Some people were rising up to meet Him in the air, but most were screaming in terror. This Man has great powers that we know nothing of, and I believe Him to be a God more powerful than any of our Roman ones. Pilate must not kill Him."

Antonia nodded. Everything the woman said made sense to her, for surely Someone who could raise a dead girl back to life again was more powerful than any of the gods revered in Rome.

Claudia dictated a hurried message to her servant. "Please take this to my husband immediately."

"But he is in judgment right how," the servant protested.

"Yes, that is why it is so important for him get this immediately. Do not let it wait until he is finished."

"As you wish." The servant bowed and departed. They waited anxiously, but received no return message.

"Petronius," Claudia announced, "there is something you could do for us. Would you please find out what is happening and let us know? With a mob that size it is dangerous for us to leave the residential quarters, but I must know what is going on."

When Petronius at last returned he looked exhausted. "It's not going well," he said. "Your husband tried to release Him. The crowd almost started a riot. The Judean leaders have threatened him with blackmail. If he does not crucify this Man—even though he has ruled that he found no fault in Him—they will accuse him of *maiesta minuta* (neglect of state duty) to Caesar."

Claudia groaned and slumped into a chair. "Caesar is so paranoid right now of anyone plotting against him that he would likely believe it," she said slowly. "Word has come that my husband's patron Sejanus has been executed for treason. That hangs as a cloud over us, and what the crowd is doing is a grave threat."

Petronius nodded. "Yes, it puts Pilate in direct danger. Then he offered, as is his custom this time of year, to release a political prisoner. He came up with the most unlikely one he could find. One that they would be the least happy to have in their midst again. Barabbas. He gave them a choice, letting this murderer loose among them again, or releasing Yeshua of Nazareth who has never hurt anyone."

"And . . ."

"They howled for Barabbas."

Claudia put her hands over her face. Antonia felt tears stinging her own eyelids. How could this be happening? The crowd's shouts were so loud they could hear them even within the thick stone walls of the fortress. By now they had worked up to a loud rhythm: "Crucify him, crucify him." Antonia's head seemed to throb with the shouts.

"And did my husband stand up to them?" Claudia asked quietly.

Petronius lowered his gaze. "Your husband called for a basin of water and washed his hands and declared the blood of this Man to be on the Judean leaders."

"Oh no," Antonia cried. "So what is to happen to Yeshua?"

"He is to be scourged and then crucified out on Golgotha," Petronius replied tonelessly.

Antonia sank to her knees, unable to stand anymore. "What can we do?"she whispered.

"Nothing, nothing," Claudia answered, her words barely audible. "Nothing."

Petronius called for water and had servants bathe the faces of the other two. "This is not a time for mourning yet, though that time is coming. We need to be strong."

"For what?" Claudia demanded. "What can we do now?"

"Well," Petronius said after a pause, "I can do nothing to prevent

His death, but I can stand by Him. I plan to go to Golgotha and stand in silence. I owe Him at least that much."

"I'll go with you," Antonia added, rising to her feet and putting her hand into Petronius'.

"Yes," Claudia said, "we will stand with Him. Come, we must change our clothes. We will go heavily veiled so that no one will know who we are."

Antonia smiled. "That will be fine, because I am sure *He* will know." And they hurried to the dressing room.

RACHEL

JERUSALEM

 n a huge sigh of frustration Rachel let out her breath. She and her family had brought Mary, mother of Yeshua, with them to Jerusalem for the Passover. Mary had heard through the city gossip that her Son was going to be there, and she was hoping to see Him. Instead, they discovered that Mary's Son was once again in trouble with the authorities. Rachel shook her head. "Yeshua has never learned how to deal respectfully with the priests, has He?" Mary just looked at her.

"I'm sorry, Mary. I know your Son means well. It's just that He never does things the easy way, does He?" Still Mary said nothing.

"They say that He has been taken back to Pilate's fortress for judgment," Rachel continued with another sigh. "Maybe if we walk toward there we will be able to find out what is happening. I'm sure Pilate isn't going to care about the wounded pride of a few priests. This will probably all be over by the time we get there, and perhaps He'll come back and spend the Passover with us."

"Perhaps," Mary said finally. "Let's go."

Crowds packed the streets. Passover was one of the annual occasions when everyone who possibly could came to Jerusalem to celebrate. Rachel grasped Mary's hand so they would not get separated as they pushed through the narrow streets. Up ahead conditions seemed worse. They heard a lot of shouting and many women wailing.

Rachel turned to a young woman heading the opposite direction. "What's going on up there?"

The woman turned to her with red-rimmed eyes. "They're killing Yeshua of Nazareth. He's to be executed at Golgotha."

Mary's eyes widened in horror.

"Are you sure you want to go?" Rachel asked Yeshua's mother. "I can take you back to the room we rented."

Mary turned to her. "Of course I want to go. He's my Son."

"Of course. That was a stupid question." Then Rachel put her arm around her friend. "He's done miracles before. Remember, He made wine out of water and raised people from the dead. The other times they've tried to kill Him nothing has happened. Once in Nazareth you said they wanted to push Him off the cliff and He just disappeared right into the crowd. I'm sure He will not let any harm come to Himself."

"Come on," Mary urged. "Let's hurry."

The two women forced their way through the noisy, angry crowd until they were near the front of the place of execution. Mary caught her breath when she first glimpsed her Son. Rachel suppressed a cry. They hardly recognized Yeshua. Dried blood matted

His hair and some type of crown of briers stabbed into his flesh. His face was puffy and discolored with bruises. The soldiers were pulling His clothes off, getting ready to bind Him to the cross. The skin on His back looked shredded. "They've scourged Him," Rachel said in horror.

Then she squeezed Mary's hand and whispered, "Miracles. It's going to be all right." Both women watched expectantly. The soldiers had tied the other two men to be executed to their crosses. Now they threw Mary's Son down on the cross, but instead of binding Him with ropes they brought large metal spikes.

Rachel bit her lip. Crucifixions were usually done with rope. The Romans used spikes and nailed criminals to crosses only when they wanted to make a special example of them and increase their suffering. As if hanging in the Judean sun, unable to breathe without pulling yourself up, was not agony enough.

When the soldiers placed the spikes and pounded them through His bleeding flesh, Rachel grabbed Mary just as she sank to the ground in a faint.

Antonia

laudia and Antonia were dressed as local Judeans and were about to leave when Pilate strode into the room. He took a second look at them and then burst into laughter. "What are you doing?" he asked.

Claudia gazed at him coolly. "No, what have *you* done, my husband?"

"What do you mean?"

"You know what I mean. I sent a message to you pleading for you to have nothing to do with Yeshua. You even admitted He was faultless. How could you do this?"

Pilate shrugged, though he also seemed defensive at being confronted by his wife. "What did you want me to do?" Anger began to tinge his voice. "I felt sorry for the man, and he's obviously not a criminal, but the priests were blackmailing me. They threatened to tell Caesar that I was guilty of neglecting my duty. It was hardly worth risking my entire career and perhaps my life for some poor Judean who was almost dead as it was."

He spread his hands in exasperation. "You should have seen him. That rabble had dragged him around all night. I understand the priests interrogated him at least twice. Their Sanhedrin examined Him twice, and he'd been twice here to me and once to visit Herod Antipas. By then he looked terrible. You know it's standard procedure to have a prisoner scourged. After that I let the soldiers amuse themselves with him. He was practically dead. I thought surely that if I brought him out in front of the mob then, they would feel sorry for him and let him crawl off and die in peace somewhere. But no, you should have heard them."

"We did hear them." Claudia spat the words out. "I'm sure all of Jerusalem could hear them."

"Exactly. So what did you expect me to do? Cross that deranged mob and trigger another uprising? We can't afford to be recalled to Rome."

"You condemned Him to death," she repeated numbly. "You had a choice."

Struggling to control his anger, Pilate shrugged. "Well, I did tell them to put a sign over His head that announcing Him "King of the Jews."

Claudia was silent for a moment and then said, "He isn't just their King—He's the Messiah of their God, too."

They stared at each other for several moments; then Claudia turned to Antonia. "Come, we have a choice too, and I choose to stand with Him."

Antonia moved to her side. Pilate exhaled in defeat and frustration. "Well," he said to Petronius, "if they want to meddle in Judean affairs, at least make sure they don't get killed or recognized."

SARAH

GOLGOTHA

 arah stood supporting Mary, formerly of Magdala, on one side; Martha, her sister, supported her on the other side. Lazarus was not far away. Sarah and Mary had become close friends since Simon's feast. All of them were horrified by the violent treatment Yeshua had endured, as well as the venomous taunts hurled at Him by some of their religious leaders. But they could do nothing. They could not even weep. Their faces could not betray their feelings. The Romans might crucify anyone who showed the slightest sympathy to a victim of crucifixion. It was part of the terror their occupiers used to keep their nation in subjection.

Yeshua was bleeding and in terrible agony as He hung by the metal spikes on the cross. From time to time He would open His eyes, and now they rested on His mother. She had approached as close as she dared. His gaze moved from her face to that of His disciple, John, one of the few who hadn't fled in fear.

"Woman, behold your son," He whispered. And then to John, "Behold your mother." Even in His suffering state He showed concern for His widowed mother. John stepped forward and put his arm around Mary, who laid her head on his shoulder.

Next to them was a tall man with curly red hair holding a small child who had the same red hair. The little one started to cry. "I'm hungry, Father. When are we going to leave?"

"Shh," his father whispered. "I can't leave. Not yet."

"But I'm hungry," wailed the little one.

Martha frowned. She turned to the redheaded man. "You should be ashamed of yourself," she said. "This is no place to bring a little child, and he's hungry."

David turned and looked at her. Sarah glanced at Mary. They couldn't believe Martha was speaking to a strange man. No self-respecting Jewish woman would do that. They both shook their heads.

"Where is his mother, anyway?" Martha demanded.

The man calmly turned to her and said, "The child has no mother. She died when he was born. He goes with me everywhere, and I just can't leave. Yeshua of Nazareth healed me of leprosy."

Martha's mouth dropped open and her eyes softened. "He raised my brother from the dead," she whispered. As the child continued to cry, she said, "Here, let me take him." David started to protest, but although his son was afraid of strangers and would cling to his father like a leech, now he reached toward the dark-haired woman. Martha scooped him into her arms and held him close, burying her face in his curly mop of hair. "Little one," she said. "I just happen to have some dried fruit and some bread in my bag here. Would you like some?"

"His name is Jonathan," his father volunteered.

Martha smiled at the child. "Here, have something to eat. Your father isn't going to be ready to leave for a while."

As the 4-year-old snuggled in her arms happily munching, Martha looked up and made eye contact with Yeshua. "I'll take care of him," she whispered, then added, "I'll take care of them both."

Sarah, who had seen and heard all this, glanced at David but he didn't seem to have heard anything. The child laid his head on Martha's shoulder and closed his eyes. Sarah prayed he would fall asleep and not remember anything about the day.

I couldn't help hoping the same thing. Martha was right. This was no place for a child. Yet I was glad the child was there, for it gave Martha someone to focus on and take care of. She was most comfortable that way. And I would not be at all surprised if this meeting of two who loved Yeshua of Nazareth would not end in another plan. The Almighty was like that even at the most difficult times, still watching out and caring for the needs and feelings and relationships of His humans.

Antonia

GOLGOTHA

ntonia stood with Claudia staring in shock at the execution. Longenius was the centurion in charge, but her father had come and now stood with him as if to keep him company. Yet Antonia knew her father well enough to know that he was there to support his friend who was having to supervise the crucifixion of One he had accepted as the Messiah.

The soldiers finished nailing Yeshua of Nazareth to the cross and tilted it forward into a standing position, then dropped it with a sickening thud into the hole carved in the rock for that purpose. It jarred a groan from Yeshua. Leaning His head back, He whispered, "Father, forgive them, for they know not what they do."

Antonia fought the tears welling up in her eyes. Yeshua forgave even His executioners. She saw her father and Longenius exchange glances; then her father strode over and grabbed a flask from one of the soldiers. Longenius raised one eyebrow. "Are you going to drug Him?"

Her father nodded. Antonia was relieved. The drink consisted of wine vinegar with bitter gall added. It dulled the pain and numbed the mind. Perhaps it would lessen Yeshua's suffering and make Him oblivious to the insults hurled at Him by the crowd. Yet when her father put it to Yeshua's lips, He jerked His head to one side, refusing it.

"Why?" Claudia asked, turning to Antonia. "Why won't He drink it?"

They looked on in confusion. But I understood perfectly. Even in His tortured state He was still God as well as man and could still choose not to suffer the humiliation, indignities, and physical abuse. He *could* decide to come down from the cross just as the taunting priests encouraged Him to. Thus He needed His mind as clear as possible not to give in to the temptation. Yeshua must complete the plan He and His Father had devised so long before.

THAD

ome on, Thad," his father said as they got up from the spot where they had been resting by the road. "We can't stop too long. We need to get to Jerusalem before sundown."

Thad nodded. He was delighted to be going to Jerusalem for his first Passover with his father. Most boys did this when they turned 12. Thad hadn't had that opportunity, because when he was 12 his father had been running around the cemetery like a wild animal. But Yeshua of Nazareth had healed him, sending the demons into the local herd of pigs. Though it had terrified and angered the townspeople of the Decapolis, Yeshua of Nazareth had restored Thad's father to him and given him a life again. Now he would get to go to Jerusalem and celebrate Passover just like other Jewish boys.

As they crested a rocky ridge, Thad pointed toward Jerusalem. "Father, what is that?"

His father squinted. "It looks like a very large thundercloud."

"But thunderclouds are in the sky. This looks like it's resting right on the ground."

"Yes, that's where Jerusalem should be. It's as if the city is covered with a thick, dark cloud."

The boy shuddered. "Maybe it's a bad omen."

"We don't believe in omens," his father said, though his voice carried a note of uncertainty. "But I really don't like the looks of it. Let's go see what's happening there."

"Are you sure we ought to? We've waited this long; maybe we should attend Passover next year."

His father laughed. "Oh, come now; how bad can it be?"

I shook my head. *Much worse than anything he could imagine,* I thought. It was as if the Almighty had said, "Enough. I can't bear to watch My Son suffering any longer," and pulled a cloak of darkness around Him to give Him privacy for His last hours of agony. It certainly put an end to the shouting and jeering. Many of the people in the crowds around the cross fearfully made their way back toward the city. Others stayed to see what would happen next, or to stand in support of their dying Friend.

Samuel

HEROD'S PALACE, JERUSALEM

amuel had never felt so depressed. It was the afternoon of the Passover and he was stuck in Herod's kitchen and resenting every minute of it. The boy had been discouraged ever since the execution of the prophet who baptized at Jordan. John had affirmed Yeshua of Nazareth as the Messiah, and now He had been arrested too.

Rumors had reached Samuel of what had taken place when the Roman governor sent the Teacher to Herod. Herod's court had come to Jerusalem for the yearly feast, and Pilate seemed to want to mend fences with the client ruler. What was happening? Why wasn't God paying attention? Could John and Yeshua of Nazareth have been false prophets? Did God just not care about them?

As Samuel turned his doubts over and over in his mind, the room suddenly became dark. "Hey, what happened?" he blurted out. It was only afternoon. The sun should still be up. What could it be? Fear filled the voices of the other people in the kitchen. It was so dark Samuel could not even see his hand in front of his face. He felt along the walls to the door and out into the courtyard. But it was black as night in the courtyard, too. Cries of terror spread throughout the palace. Above them all Samuel could hear Herod's bellowing. The boy smiled to himself. Maybe God was paying attention after all. Perhaps this was part of His plan to save Yeshua of Nazareth from execution.

Sadly I shook my head. Samuel was so hopeful, yet he did not understand the plan or how God was carrying it out.

ANDREW

GOLGOTHA

Instinctively Andrew reached for his mother in the darkness. It was his job to protect her, and in a mob like this anything could happen even if it wasn't dark. When he pulled her close to him, she whispered, "It's so dark. Do you think Yeshua of Nazareth did that?"

"I don't know," he whispered back, "but maybe He really will come down from the cross now, as the priests have been telling Him to. Wouldn't that fix them?"

"I don't think He's coming down," the boy's mother continued. "I think He's dying."

"No," Andrew protested. "He won't die. He's already shown His power over death. He's stronger than death. Yeshua woke me up from it, remember? He won't die."

"I hope not." Suddenly they heard a strangled cry from the cross. "He's saying something."

Then Yeshua cleared his throat and spoke louder. "Eloi, Eloi, lama sabachthani?"

"He's calling for Elias," someone said from behind Andrew.

And then over to one side: "Let's see if Elias comes and helps Him out of this one."

Andrew frowned. It didn't sound as if He was asking for Elias, but the boy couldn't make out the words. He kept turning the phrase over in his mind. At last he decided "Eloi, Eloi" was "My God, My God," and the rest seemed to be "Why have You forsaken Me?"

Of course, it was the beginning of a psalm, a psalm of David. Andrew started whispering the words as well as he could remember them. "'My God, My God, why have You deserted Me? Why do You seem to be so far away when I need You to save Me? Why do You seem so far away that You can't hear My groans? My God, I cry out in the daytime, but You don't answer. I cry out at night, I can't keep quiet.'"

The boy paused, then began chanting the words out loud: "'But You rule from Your throne as the Holy One. You are the God Israel praises. Our people of long ago put their trust in You. They trusted in You and You saved them. They cried out to You and were saved. They trusted in You and You didn't let them down.'"

As his confidence grew Andrew began to speak even louder.

"'People treat Me like a worm and not a man. They hate Me and look down on Me. All those who see Me laugh at Me. They shout at Me and make fun of Me. They shake their heads at Me. They say, "He trusts in the Lord. Let the Lord help Him. If the Lord is pleased with Him, let Him save Him."'"

Suddenly Andrew swallowed hard. How did the psalmist know exactly what they would be saying here today? Perhaps that was why Yeshua had quoted the psalm. "'But You brought Me out of My mother's body,'" the boy continued. "'You made Me trust in You even when I was at My mother's breast. From the time I was born You took good care of Me. Ever since I came out of My mother's body, You have been My God. Don't be far away from Me. Trouble is near and there is no one to help Me. My enemies are all around Me. They are like strong bulls from the land of Bashan. They are like roaring lions that tear to pieces what they kill. They open their mouths wide to attack Me.'" *That's for sure,* Andrew thought. "'My strength is like water that is poured out on the ground. I feel as if My bones aren't connected.'"

For a moment Andrew stopped and pondered what he had been reciting. Yeshua probably did feel exactly as if His blood was dribbling out of Him like water poured on the ground. And hanging there, His joints would seem pulled apart.

The boy continued to recite the psalm. "'My heart has turned to wax. It has melted away inside of Me. My strength is dried up like a piece of broken pottery. My tongue sticks to the roof of My mouth. You bring Me down to the edge of the grave. A group of sinful people has closed in on Me. They are all around Me like a pack of dogs. They have pierced My hands and My feet. I can see all of My bones right through My skin. People stare at Me and laugh when I suffer. They divide up My clothes among them. They cast lots for what I am wearing.'"

A second voice joined Andrew—his mother. "'Lord, don't be so far away. You give Me strength. Come quickly to help Me. Save Me from the sword. Save the only life I have. Save Me from the power of those dogs. Save Me from the mouth of those lions. Save Me from the horns of those wild oxen. I will announce Your name to My brothers and sisters. I will praise You among those who worship You. You who have respect for the Lord, praise Him. All you people of Jacob honor Him. All you people of Israel worship Him. He has not forgotten the One who is hurting. He has not turned away from His suffering. He has not turned His face away from Him. He has listened to His cry for help.'"

Andrew stopped, realizing that God had heard. *He has sent this darkness. God has not turned away from Yeshua's suffering,* he thought. *The Lord is giving Him privacy and it has stopped the jeering crowd.*

Not caring what the Roman guards thought, even if they could have seen who he was, Andrew chanted even louder. "'Because of what You have done, I will praise You in the whole community of those who worship You. In front of those who respect You, I will keep My promises. Those who are poor will eat and be satisfied. Those who look to the Lord will praise Him. May their hearts be filled with new hope. People from one end of the earth to the other will remember and turn to the Lord. The people of all nations will bow down before Him. The Lord is King. He rules over nations.'"

Yeshua might not be able to breathe well enough to finish the psalm, but He had started it and Andrew was determined to finish it for Him. "'All the rich people of the earth will worship God,'" the boy continued, "'and take part in His feasts. All those who go down to the edge of the grave will fall on their knees in front of Him. I'm talking about those who can hardly keep themselves alive. Those who are not yet born will serve Him. Those who are born later will be told about the Lord, and they will tell people who have not yet been born that He has done what is right.'"

As Andrew finished the psalm, his mother squeezed his arm.

For centuries to come, those who did not know their Scriptures would think that Yeshua was agonizing that God was forsaking Him. But those who read their Scriptures and knew their psalms would understand that it was not a cry of defeat, but a declaration of triumph.

AฑโอฑiA Aฑด

DEBORAH

GOLGOTHA

n the darkness Antonia felt a hand on her shoulder and a familiar whisper. "Antonia, is that you?" She started and spun around but could see no one in the thick darkness.

"It's me, Deborah."

"Deborah, how did you find me here?"

"I saw you earlier, but I wasn't sure it was you from the way you're dressed. But the crowd was too thick for me to get to you, so I've been trying to find you in the darkness here as people thinned out. Isn't this terrible?"

The Roman girl nodded, but then realized Deborah couldn't see her, and said, "Yes, I feel just sick."

"Me too," her friend agreed. "But I guess there's nothing we can do now except stay with Him. It seems so little after all He did for us."

"I know, but I believe that at least He knows we're here. He's been so quiet in the darkness for a while now." The darkness had lifted over the city but still clung around the cross.

"Listen to His breathing," Deborah suddenly whispered.

Antonia did. Yeshua's breathing was much faster now. Rapid, gasping, deep breaths. As flashes of lightning now illuminated the cross, they could see His drooping head. Suddenly a bright light shown right on Yeshua's face. He lifted His head and cried out, "It is finished!" It was a cry not of defeat, but triumph. "Into Thy hands I commend My spirit," He declared.

As a huge clap of thunder shook the city, Yeshua bowed His head and His whole body sagged. Another clap of thunder. Was it thunder? Even the ground was shaking. "It's an earthquake!" Deborah exclaimed. It was as if the whole earth was shuddering as Yeshua died. Priests and others who had been shouting and jeering now lay trembling on the ground, unable to keep their balance as the ground reeled.

"Father!" Antonia shouted.

She heard her father's voice close by. "Surely this was the Son of God." When she reached toward the sound of his voice, he scooped her up in his strong arms and held her close. The blood that had been dribbling down the cross and pooling on the rock below now poured into the broken and cracked rock and soaked into the earth.

LEVI

lthough the crucifixion of Yeshua of Nazareth just outside the city walls had stirred up much excitement, Levi was unable to go and see what was happening for it was his day for duty for the Passover. He stood near the altar, bringing water for the priests. They were having to perform the sacrifice of the Passover lamb by torchlight because of the darkness. As the priest raised the knife, the earthquake suddenly hit. The whole Temple rocked and rumbled as if it were about to fall on them and crush them all. The lamb slipped away from the priest's grasp and ran bleating through the courtyard and disappeared into the crowd of worshipers.

Behind the priest the huge curtain that separated the holy from the Most Holy Place began to rip. A cry went up from the people watching at the gateway to the inner courtyard as they realized it was being torn from top to bottom. No human hands could have done that; the curtain was way too high.

Levi stared at the emptiness and shuddered. Apart from the fact that God was not there, the curtain was torn open and anyone could stare into it. Levi suddenly realized that the presence of God with Israel was Yeshua, and He was being crucified.

We have to stop them! he thought, and yet he knew that the darkness and the earthquake indicated that it was too late. He fell on his knees in the courtyard of the Temple as it continued to shake and rumble. "O God of Abraham, Isaac and Jacob, God of Yeshua of Nazareth, forgive us. Forgive us for being so slow to understand. Forgive us for killing our Messiah. O Father of Israel, what have we done?" And he burst into tears.

MARK

GOLGOTHA, PASSOVER

I hovered above the scene, trying to take it all in. Even though I knew all the prophecies and had witnessed everything up to this point, I just couldn't believe that the evil one would really do this to the Son of God. Now I couldn't bring myself even to say his name. None of us called him Lucifer anymore. Son of the morning, the brightest star in the angelic choir—how could he have sunk to this?

We didn't always understand the conflict between him and the Most High. Until now we had had to make our choices of loyalty without knowing all the details and without grasping how it was going to turn out. Even though we didn't understand, I and my fellow guardians and recorders, cherubim and seraphim, had chosen to remain loyal to the Most High while others had gone with the evil one.

The things he was willing to do to humans horrified us. Shedding human blood was bad enough, but now he had spilled the blood of the Son of the Most High. We may not have always understood the implications of the cosmic struggle and we may have felt sorry for Satan at one time, but *now* there was no question in anyone's mind.

In the beginning the deceiver had claimed that there could be no forgiveness for humanity, that according to God's own laws He could not forgive them because they had sinned. All of a sudden it was clear to me why the Almighty had allowed Satan and his rebellion to continue this long. It had gone on for humanity's sake, for there could not have been forgiveness and salvation for the human race without this sacrifice. And allowing the deceiver to have his way so long forever removed any question in anyone's mind, whether angel or human—once they understood what had happened here today.

From the beginning Satan had lied to humans. He had caused them to fear the very Being who loved them more than anyone else in the universe did. If they could only see, if they could just grasp what had taken place here today. The evil one had known God, had experienced His unending depths of love. He had no excuse. Yet surely if humans could see today's events, they wouldn't be able to resist such love and such compassion. Still I wondered if future humans would regard this day as a triumph of the Most High. Would they look at this as the purchase of their freedom, the greatest act of love ever committed in the entire universe, or would Satan lie to them once again and have them just view this with panic and guilt as they realized that their sins had made such a sacrifice necessary?

I vowed that I would do everything in my power to help them understand the significance of what really had happened here today, to let humans know that the Son of God did not die on Calvary to make them feel guilty for their sins, but that God gave His Son so that they didn't have to feel bad anymore—ever.

SARAH

arah let go of Mary Magdalene's hand as the darkness cleared. Cautiously checking to see if any of the Roman guards were looking her way, she took a step toward the cross. "He's not breathing anymore," she said quietly. Mary started to wail, but Sarah clamped her hand over the other woman's mouth. "Shh. There will be time for that later. What can we do?"

Mary collected herself, threw back her shoulders, and drew herself up to her full height. "We have to find a way to get His body," she said. "I have a tomb made empty by Yeshua Himself. Our family burial chamber where Lazarus was not too long ago. To shame us the Romans won't let us have the bodies of those they crucify, but perhaps we can steal Yeshua's body if they leave it on the cross. We must make a plan."

Slowly Sarah shook her head. "I don't think we can do that. There are too many people here who would not want us to get Him."

"Keep thinking," Mary persisted. "We must think of a plan."

ELIHU BEN MALCHUS

s the two women discussed Jesus' body Elihu stood behind them. Not far from him watched two wealthy members of the Sanhedrin: Joseph of Arimathaea and Nicodemus. Elihu knew who they were because his father had told him about them. Both of them were moderates who had advised against violence toward Yeshua of Nazareth during previous discussions. Later the ruling body had carefully excluded them from the high priest's meetings and the gathering of the Sanhedrin the night before when Yeshua had been brought before them for judgment. Both men had been afraid to speak out too strongly in the past. Now fear no longer held them back.

"You know the Roman procedure," Nicodemus said to Joseph. "They let the bodies hang on the cross until they rot. Even to ask for a victim's body is to invite our own immediate execution. The best we can hope for Him is a criminal's burial."

"Yes, yes," Joseph said, ignoring the danger, "but He's not a criminal. Pilate said so himself."

"So what are you proposing?"

"Well, why don't I talk to Pilate?"

"Pilate?" Nicodemus echoed.

"Yes, Pilate. I'd rather not deal with Caiaphas or Annas."

"You're right; you're better off with Pilate. And I'll buy some spices to embalm Him."

Elihu stared in amazement. He wondered if Joseph and Nicodemus would meet the same fate as their Master had.

Antonia

s soon as the earthquake stopped, Antonia's father had growled, "Petronius, this is no place for my daughter. Get her back to the fortress immediately."

"Yes sir," Petronius said, and then glanced meaningfully toward Claudia. Antonia's father glanced at the woman, then stared.

"Oh," he stammered. "My lady, I did not realize it was you."

"You weren't supposed to," she replied. "That's why we're dressed like this. Petronius, take us back to the fortress."

The Roman servant hurried them back up toward Jerusalem. As they entered the residential portion of the fortress, they realized they weren't alone. Joseph of Arimathaea was talking with Pilate.

"How can that be?" Pilate demanded. "And why hasn't anyone told me? No one dies of crucifixion in only six hours."

"Well," Joseph replied cautiously, "He had been scourged and suffered much other abuse during the night."

"Yes, I suppose so," Pilate said, calming a little, "but I just have never heard of anyone dying in only six hours. The whole point of crucifixion is to keep the victim . . . Never mind. Why didn't anyone tell me?" He paced back and forth, shouting at the guards. They wisely did not answer.

After patiently waiting for Pilate to cool down, the Judean leader continued. "The issue of how He died within six hours is not as important to me as what happens next. I am concerned about His body. I wish to bury Him."

The Roman official glared at them. "You know our policy."

The Judean bowed and remained silent. Pilate studied him and seemed to be lost in thought. Finally he declared, "So bury Him. What is that to me? I'm not a Judean."

"According to law, anyone who is executed for treason must have a criminal's burial."

"Are you here representing the priests and the Sanhedrin?"

"No, sir."

"You are a disciple of His?"

Joseph stared at the floor, then replied, "I have been a cowardly disciple until now. Although I did not support Him during His life, I will support Him now. I have a new tomb that has never been used, and wish to give Him a burial fit for the most noble Judean in all the country. I would be honored if I could bury Him there."

Pilate chuckled. "And suppose I did release His body to you? That would irritate your Temple leaders, wouldn't it?"

"Yes, sir," Joseph answered slowly.

Making a decision, the Roman official snapped, "Take His body. Give Him a royal burial. After all," he said with a smirk, "He is the King of the Jews." Antonia looked at Pilate's wife.

Elihu ben Malchus

lihu looked up as he saw the two wealthy men hurrying toward the foot of the cross. He edged closer, trying to hear their conversation with the centurions, but he couldn't make out the words. Then the heavier of the two men pulled a parchment from his sleeve and handed it to the centurion who broke the seal and opened it and read the instructions.

"All right," the Roman officer said to his men, "let's take Him down."

"No," a nearby priest shouted. "Absolutely not."

The centurion turned and stood with his legs wide apart, his arms crossed against his chest. "No? Are you overruling an order from Pilate, or did I misunderstand you? We could replace Him with you."

"Ah, no, that is, yes, I mean yes, you misunderstood me," the priest stammered. "Did Pilate say He would be allowed to be buried?"

"He's dead," the centurion pointed out sarcastically.

"Are you sure He's dead?" asked the priest suspiciously.

"Are you suggesting that after years of being a soldier I can't tell a dead man from a live one?" the centurion replied softly, resting his hand on the hilt of his sword.

"No, no, I—I wouldn't be implying that."

"So now may we have permission to go ahead with Pilate's orders?" the centurion sneered.

"Certainly," the priest stammered, stepping back.

SARAH

arah kept her arm firmly around Mary Magdalene's waist to support her as the disciple John held Mary, Yeshua's mother. Joseph of Arimathaea and Nicodemus took Yeshua down from the cross. After wrapping His limp body carefully in a linen sheet with expensive embalming spices that Nicodemus had bought, they carried it to Joseph's new tomb, which fortunately was not far from the crucifixion site.

At the tomb three of the disciples unwrapped the linen enough to straighten Yeshua's limbs and pull the matted hair back from His face. They folded His hands on His chest.

"We'll come back early in the morning on Sunday," Sarah suggested.

"I just hate to leave Him here," Yeshua's mother cried.

* * *

The next day a group of soldiers marched into the garden. "Whose idea was this?" one soldier asked. "We're usually not asked to guard people as cooperative as this one is going to be." He gestured toward the tomb.

"It's what the priests want, and Pilate seems to want to make them happy, so we're going to stand here and guard him so he doesn't run away in the night," one of the other soldiers replied.

The first soldier nodded in a bored way.

The soldiers wasted no time in attaching a large Roman seal to the tomb. Now it would be breaking the law to enter it or to touch the body of Yeshua of Nazareth.

Elihu ben Malchus

sually Elihu loved Passover. Everyone came to Jerusalem, and Sabbath was the best. But there was no joy in the celebrations this year. Even though the sun was shining and the Temple looked dazzling as usual, it seemed as if a dark pall hung over everyone. The priests mumbled nervously to one another, and everyone on Temple duty was especially jumpy.

"Elihu," barked a familiar voice. The boy jumped and turned.

"Yes sir," he answered, bowing his head respectfully. It was Caiaphas, the high priest himself.

"How is your father doing?"

"He is still resting at home," the boy answered.

"Is his ear healing?"

"Oh yes, his ear is perfect. Yeshua of Nazareth reattached it and it is just . . ."

"Yes, yes, yes," Caiaphas interrupted. "I know the story. So what is his problem?"

"He says it is his stomach," the boy answered carefully.

"My stomach hasn't been well since then either. Well, tell him to take whatever remedy he requires to get back on the job. I need him back as soon as possible. The people are very restless. Many of them brought their sick, hoping to be healed by that Nazarene, and they are angry that he has been executed."

Elihu had heard people discussing it as he had watched the crowds coming and going.

"If that isn't bad enough," the high priest continued, "apparently he had circulated some rumors among his followers about how he would arise on the third day after his death. This is not good. The other members of the Sanhedrin are meeting with us this afternoon to decide what to do about it. I really need your father. He runs my household, and without him, especially at a time like this, the other servants are nervous. We've had several disappear," he said confidentially.

The boy bowed. "I will give him your message, sir."

"Good, and be quick about it." Turning abruptly, he walked back toward the Temple.

Elihu took a deep breath and headed for home.

SARAH

GARDEN OF JOSEPH OF ARIMATHAEA, PASSOVER SUNDAY

arah had not slept much. How could she after all that had happened? She and Mary Magdalene had gotten up since they couldn't sleep anyway. Mary still had a fair amount of money left over from her past life. She and Sarah had gone to the market and bought as much embalming perfume as Mary could afford. Now they crept out toward Joseph of Arimathaea's garden through the darkness. The terrain was rough, so they held on to each other as they walked, but said nothing. They had nothing left to say after the events of the past few days, but they both sensed that they were closer as friends than they had ever been.

Tremors still shook the ground, and on their way to the garden another one rippled the earth. Both women fell to the ground and lay there clinging to each other.

"Mary, do you think the world is coming to an end?"

"I don't know," she whispered. "It may be that the earth is angry because we humans have killed the Messiah." When the shaking stopped, they stood on their wobbly legs and gathered up their perfume and belongings to continue toward the tomb.

"What are we going to do when we get there?" Sarah asked. "That stone they rolled in front of the grave is heavier than we can move, and I heard that Pilate had the soldiers seal it. You know what that means."

"Maybe they just sealed it with cords," Mary suggested.

"Maybe. Do you suppose if we ask them really nicely . . . ?"

"Let me do that," Mary suggested. "I'm good at that. I may be able to talk them into rolling the stone back and allowing us to enter. After we finish we can get the soldiers to put the stone back before it's light."

"Do you think they will let us?"

Mary shrugged. "I don't know. But if anyone can talk them into it, it should be me."

As they came in sight of the garden tomb they stared in shock. The stone had been flung to the side, and the soldiers were gone.

"No," Mary shrieked. She turned and fled.

"Wait for me," her friend called, but Mary had vanished. Unsure of the way back to where they were staying, Sarah found a little nook and hid in the bushes. What had happened at the tomb? Could someone have taken Yeshua's body? Was it the final insult to His memory? She sat quietly, not understanding, as the tears rolled down her cheeks. Surely someone else that she might know would come to the garden soon and help her find her way back. In the meantime, she would just wait. If she couldn't be near Yeshua, the next best thing was to be near where He had been last. Resting her head on her arms, she burst into more sobs.

It wasn't long before she heard footsteps and whispers. A few streaks of light dotted the eastern sky, but it was still dark. She pulled her cloak up over her head so that only her eyes were peeking out. In the darkness and with the foliage, perhaps no one would notice her. As the visitors rounded the corner so that she could see who they were, they screamed in astonishment.

I had been waiting for them—or anyone who would come close enough to the tomb. Heaven had given me permission to materialize, and I sat on the right side of the tomb entrance, ready to explain what had happened. Even though I am not one of the warriors or guardians, the people acted just as frightened at the sight of me. I tried to comfort them and spoke loud enough that I hoped Sarah could hear it from her hiding place.

"Don't be afraid," I said. "I know what you're here for. You're looking for Yeshua, who was crucified. He isn't here, but His body was not stolen. He's alive. He's risen! Come, look." They took a few steps into the tomb. "See, here is the cloth He was wrapped in, and here is the napkin that was over His face."

Mary the mother of James reached out and rubbed the material between her fingers. "This is the cloth," she said. "Look, Salome. Remember Friday, when Joseph brought this over? We both felt it because it's such high-quality linen. The weave is . . ."

"Yes, yes," Salome interrupted. "Who cares about the weaving? Where is Yeshua?"

Patiently I smiled and answered, "He is alive and you will see Him, but right now go back and tell the other disciples and Peter that He has left here. He's heading for Galilee, and you should go there too. He'll meet you there."

"Peter?" Salome questioned. "You know that none of us are really talking to him right now."

I nodded. "Yeshua wants you to tell Peter, too. Please tell the disciples and Peter to meet Him in Galilee."

"Oh," Mary gasped, "Peter will be so relieved. He's feeling terrible."

"He ought to," Salome snapped.

Finally my message sank in. They turned to each other. "Let's go tell them!" they shouted and ran from the tomb.

I shook my head. Sarah couldn't follow them back either, for they were gone before she realized what had happened. She still continued to crouch in the bushes, not knowing what to do. But I was there with her, along with many others whom she just couldn't see.

Light was starting to pour across the horizon. It was going to be a good day.

* * *

Sarah felt as if she had been crouching in the bushes for hours when she again heard feet pounding down the path. She huddled closer to the ground. It did not sound like the approach of any of her friends. First John arrived, and then Peter. The women must have told the disciples. She had heard that Peter had been frightened and had denied that he even knew Yeshua during the trial, but then many people had been frightened. She made a wry face as she remembered how it was mostly the women who had remained with Yeshua right to the end. Perhaps that was because women had so much less to lose, already being fairly low in social status.

She watched as Peter stooped and entered the tomb. Then John pushed in next to Peter. "Look!" he cried. "Here is the linen that He was wrapped in. It's all folded and His face cloth is here at the end."

"Is it the same cloth?" Peter questioned. "Could it be a fake?"

"No," said John. "Look at this. There is dried blood everywhere it touched Him."

Peter nodded. "Yes, this is the cloth."

They came out slowly. Sarah strained to hear the voice that had talked to the women, but she heard nothing.

"I can't believe it. He really isn't here," Peter said. "He must be alive!"

"Well, that's what the women said," John replied.

"Do you think we can really believe them?" Peter asked hesitantly. "I mean, after all we've been through the past few days. Do you think they really saw an angel? Did he really talk to them?"

Sarah wanted to shout at them, to tell them what idiots they were. Just because they hadn't seen it they assumed it must not be true. But something made her wait silently instead.

"I don't know, I don't know," Peter kept repeating and shaking his head. "I want to believe it. The angel said they should tell me, too."

John put his arm around his shoulders. "He's not angry at you, Peter. He understands."

Peter's chin started to quiver. "I know, but I was just so sure that I would be loyal to Him to the end—and look at me. He deserved better friends than me."

"Well, He doesn't want better friends than you. He wants *you,* or He wouldn't have asked the angel to tell the women that. Now come on. Let's go get our things packed up and head for Galilee. He'll find us. The Master knows where to find us. Let's go home."

Sarah started to stand up. Surely Peter and John would take her back to where the women were, but they turned and ran down the path. The girl burst into tears. "How am I ever going to get back? I've got to ask for help from whoever comes here next."

It seemed like only moments later that she heard slow footsteps on the path. She still continued to crouch, wanting to make sure it was someone friendly. Recognizing Mary Magdalene, she was just ready to stand up when someone else approached the woman.

Mary stood sobbing in front of the entrance of the tomb. "Woman, why are you crying?" a deep voice asked. "May I help you?"

"They took my Lord away," she answered, still blinded by her tears. "The tomb is empty. Look. I don't know where they put Him," she sobbed.

In her hiding place Sarah nodded to herself. Mary had run back to the disciples before the others had seen the angel. The sister of Martha and Lazarus continued to sob and hiccup. "If this tomb was too important for Him or if they wanted it for someone else, just show me where they hid His body and I'll take it away. I have a tomb back home that's empty right now."

She babbled on as the man stood there next to her. "My parents died a long time ago and their bones have been put in the ossuary boxes in the side. We had the tomb all ready again because my brother died a few months ago. But when we put him in there Yeshua of Nazareth raised him, and my brother is as alive as we are right now. So we have a place, and I would be happy to take Him there. I have money. I'll give you whatever you want if you show me where He is."

When she finally stopped for breath the deep voice said, "Mary."

Sarah jumped. She recognized the voice. Suddenly Mary turned to the stranger.

"Oh! It's You!" she shouted, reaching for Him.

"No," said Yeshua. "Don't touch Me. I still have to go to My Father, but please go back to the others and tell them I've gone to see My Father and your Father, My God and your God, to make sure that this sacrifice was acceptable. Then I'll meet you. Go home, but don't be afraid. And don't forget to tell the others."

Suddenly He disappeared. Bursting out of the bushes, Sarah flung her arms around her friend. "It's true! It's true! It's Yeshua! The others saw an angel who told them, too! It's really true!"

The two hugged each other and danced around and around in circles. "He's alive again!" they exclaimed.

I wanted to dance with them but they wouldn't have known, for I was no longer visible to human eyes. But I laughed and swooped in circles around them. If ever there was a cause for dancing, this was it!

Antonia

ANTONIA FORTRESS, JERUSALEM, PASSOVER SUNDAY MORNING

ntonia had slept little, tossing and turning and wishing for morning. Just as the light began to shine through the window, she heard someone stirring. Rising from her sleeping mat, she pulled her robe around her. Perhaps Claudia was up and they could have breakfast together. She hoped her father's duties in Jerusalem would be over as soon as possible. The girl had never wanted to go home so badly.

"This had to be the most horrible week of my whole life," she muttered to herself. "Absolutely the worst."

The girl thought about other bad times she had had. Since she hadn't been very old when Mother died, she didn't remember it, so that didn't count. The time that Deborah had died had been pretty bad, but Yeshua had raised her, and the joy in celebrating Deborah's miraculous resurrection swept away all the sorrow she had felt when she had learned that her friend had stopped breathing and would not be with her again. With a sigh she realized that Yeshua was now gone. Nothing would ever be the same again. Life was hardly worth living.

Shuffling into the public area of the residential part of the fortress, she curled up on one of the couches. Whoever was moving around in the other room would be out soon, and she'd have some-one to talk to.

With a flurry of banging and cursing, Pilate stomped into the room. "So what do they want now?" he shouted.

"It's about Yeshua of Nazareth," a servant explained, following him. Both were unaware of the girl's presence. She slid down on the couch so they would not notice her.

"I don't ever want to discuss that with them again. What is their problem? Can't they let a man rest?"

"Do you wish me to send them away?" the servant asked.

"No, no. Tell them to get their scrawny Judean bodies in here and talk to me. This is the last time I want to hear anything about Yeshua, so they'd better say it all today."

A delegation of priests entered the room. "What is the matter with you?" Pilate demanded as he looked from one to another. "You look as if you've been run over by a herd of camels."

"Or worse," one of the priests muttered. "It's Yeshua of Nazareth."

"I'm tired of hearing about him. I let you crucify him, I let you seal him in a tomb. What is your problem now?"

"He's gone," the high priest exploded.

"Gone?" Pilate asked incredulously.

"The, um, the soldiers—we need to discuss them."

"Well, I suppose we do. If they let someone in to steal the body, they'll be executed."

"Well, that's what we have to talk about," the priests replied. "We have paid them a great deal of money to say exactly *that* happened, and we promised them we would clear it with you."

The Roman official stared at them. "What are you talking about? I can understand bribery; it's what greases the wheels of government. But accepting a bribe to say that you committed a capital offense—I hardly believe that my soldiers would do that."

Antonia's stomach twisted into a knot. Roman soldiers were tough, and they were loyal. The Roman Empire would tolerate nothing else. Soldiers who slept on the job or were found to be corrupt were executed without a second thought. Could Father have been involved in this? Was his life in danger? Antonia had felt such hatred for the priests on Friday that she didn't think she could dislike them any more than she already did, but now she felt new waves of anger sweeping over her.

After standing in silence for several moments, Pilate sat down. "Tell me. What has happened?"

"You know that big earthquake this morning?" one of the priests began.

"It's been quaking the past few days, but the one this morning was almost as big as the one on Friday. I was afraid it was going to topple this fortress."

Antonia shuddered as she imagined tons of rock falling in on them.

"Well, apparently," one of the priests continued, "during that earthquake the tomb was opened. The story is that Yeshua of Nazareth came out of the tomb at that time. We have paid the soldiers to say they were sleeping when the body disappeared, because this is obviously not a story we want spread around to stir up his many followers. Besides, it would make you look bad. You're the one who ordered his crucifixion."

"Me?" Pilate glared. "Don't you remember insisting that I should crucify him?"

The priests shrugged politely. "Perhaps, but everyone knows we have no authority to order an execution. You're the only one who could have done that."

"So He's alive?" Claudia said, stepping into the room.

Everyone turned toward her. "Well," the leader of the priests replied, "we don't know that for sure, but the soldiers . . ."

"So He's alive now and you're terrified of what could happen."

"Get out," Pilate interrupted his wife, glaring at the Judean leaders. "Get out of my fortress and don't come back to talk to me about this man again. I want the soldiers here immediately."

"But sir, remember that we paid them a great deal of money to put their lives on the line and this isn't . . ."

"Get out," he shouted.

As they left, Pilate turned to his wife. "You were right," he said. "This was a terrible mistake."

She nodded. "So what are you going to do?"

"Well, first I need to find out if he is really alive."

"Will you go to Him?" Antonia asked, at last breaking her silence. "He's forgiven others."

Pilate shook his head. "My child, how can I, a Roman governor, ask forgiveness for doing my job? I think not."

"The soldiers you requested are here, sir," a servant announced, entering the room.

"Send them in."

Antonia searched their faces. No, her father was not among them. He must have been on duty somewhere else. She gave a sigh of relief.

"So what happened?" Pilate demanded. The soldiers all stared at each other in terror.

The Roman official glared at them, then suddenly, and with an expression of exhaustion, sank into a chair. "Here's the deal. The priests have already been here. They told me they bribed you to say that his body was stolen. They explained that it had something to do with the earthquake. I'm not going to execute you. I just want to know what really happened at the tomb. This superstitious country is enough to make one believe anything."

The soldiers fell on their knees. "Oh, thank you for your mercy," they said in shaking voices. "Thank you, sir; thank you."

Pilate gestured for silence. "Who is in charge here?"

One of the men stepped forward.

"What really happened?" the governor continued. "Don't make anything up; just tell it to me straight. Nothing you say will leave this room."

"We were watching the tomb," the leader said. "We were all awake and did not sleep. There were a few rumbles during the night, just small tremors, but this morning before dawn there was another large quake . . ."

"Yes, yes, I felt it here, too."

"Well," another soldier added, "it wasn't just a quake. A bright light dazed us and we all fell to the ground. We thought we were dead men."

"What was the light from?" Pilate questioned.

"It came from the tomb," the soldiers explained. "Some kind of glowing being removed the stone from the tomb entrance. Then it shouted, 'Your father calls you.' And the man who was sealed in the tomb stood and came out."

Pilate stared at them in silence for a long time. "You're sure it was him?" he asked finally.

"We're sure. He still had the wounds from his execution."

The governor sighed and rubbed his eyes. "Where did he go? What happened next?"

"We don't know. We were lying on the ground, unable to move or get up."

"He must be a god," Pilate muttered to himself.

The soldier nodded. "Yes, and in his presence we had no

strength. We were not able to move or get up until the light faded away. Although we did not see where he went, we are certain he is alive. No one took his body. He just walked away."

"Fine," Pilate said, staring at the floor. "So he's alive. And what you told me will not leave this room. You will not be executed for sleeping on duty, though if I hear of any of you ever speaking of this again, you will be. Understand?"

"Yes, sir," they answered. "Thank you, thank you."

"Now go, get out of my house and give me some peace."

The soldiers left quickly. Pilate sat with his head in his hands rocking himself back and forth, oblivious to his wife and Antonia. The girl slipped off the couch and walked over to Claudia. "He's alive!" she whispered.

Claudia flung her arms around the girl. "Yes, He's alive! He must be more powerful than the Roman gods. Executing Him didn't slow Him down. He must be the most powerful God there is."

"I feel so much better!" Antonia whispered back.

"Me too," chuckled Claudia. "Let's get something to eat; then let's find out where His followers are. Perhaps we can discover where He's gone."

"Yes, yes. Maybe we'll see Him again! I have so many things I want to ask Him." The two slipped out of the room while Pilate continued to rock back and forth with his head in his hands. He had never felt so miserable and fearful in his life.

MARK

fter the Resurrection, time seemed to fly—with the Son of the Almighty appearing in different places at various times to His followers. Some instantly responded with great rejoicing. Others harbored their doubts. How patiently He dealt with them again and again, letting people touch Him and feed Him and follow Him around, observing Him doing normal human activities and thus reassuring them that He was really there. He had so little time before His return to heaven.

As usual, His human followers continued to be oblivious to His plans or what might happen next, so He tried to prepare them. Yeshua even clearly told His disciples that He would have to leave them. But instead of asking sensible questions about things that would prepare them for that time, they just insisted that they would be going with Him.

It always amazed me how much He loved these stubborn humans. While Yeshua spent this time reassuring them and preparing them to tell everyone in the world what had happened, they continued with their lives. The fishermen were back at their job. One morning Yeshua prepared breakfast for them on the shore and spent extra time with Peter, who now loved Him more than ever before.

The Son of God appeared not only to His close personal friends, but to large crowds, even one group of 500 people. But His time was soon up. He headed toward the Mount of Olives, His disciples and many others following along. I was there too. It was easy to record several of my favorite people now as they all traveled in the group wanting to be with Him as much as they could.

On the Mount of Olives He reassured them of His love. Then He raised His hands, blessed them, and started rising into the air. Gasps of astonishment rippled through the crowd. Higher and higher He went and was soon out of sight. They could not see the clouds of angels swirling around Him, singing and shouting with excitement. For the angels the celebration was just beginning. They were accompanying Him home. I did not participate in that grand event, however. The Almighty had given me a very special assignment. One other angel and I were allowed to materialize and comfort His followers.

As He disappeared from sight and they all stood peering into the sky trying to catch one more glimpse of Him, we appeared. "Why are you humans gazing up into heaven?" we asked. "Don't be afraid and don't be discouraged, for this same Yeshua whom you love is going to come back to you in the same way as you saw Him go, with lots of clouds and angels."

We comforted them briefly, reminding them that He had promised to return to take them home, and so He would, for His commitment to humans was even stronger than any marriage between loving humans on this earth.

After the ascension David went up to Bethany with his son and his father. He had proposed marriage to Lazarus' sister Martha, and everyone in Bethany was looking forward to the wedding. As he was leaving he told Martha, "I'm going home now to prepare a place for you in our home, but I'll return so that you can be with me always." Then he paused, and they stared at each other, remembering that Yeshua had said almost those same words to them.

I smiled. Someday it would all make sense to them, and they would understand that Yeshua's commitment to them was even more beautiful than anything between a man and a woman could ever be on this planet.

I let out a great sigh. These had been some of the most exciting recording assignments I had ever received. I had watched the King of the universe give up His power and His position as well as His physical advantages to become a wobbly-necked helpless little human. I had gotten to see Him as a child and as an adult, and witnessed firsthand His love for these humans He had created.

Even more, I finally understood the great conflict that had been going on among us since before He created this planet. Until now I had never totally understood why Lucifer was so angry and why God ejected him from heaven, though I had been loyal to the Almighty from the beginning. The fallen one's vicious attacks on the Son of the Almighty here on earth had revealed his true colors. He no longer appeared as the misunderstood being that he pretended to be, but an angry, vindictive, and evil spirit who would stop at nothing to cause suffering to the Almighty and anyone loyal to Him.

None of us could have believed that he would go so far as to harm the Son of the Almighty physically, and we recoiled in horror when we saw him lead human beings to torture Yeshua of Nazareth to death. Nor could we have imagined that Yeshua's love for the weak and frightened people on this tiny planet was so great that He would allow Himself to be treated that way. It was beyond our comprehension until we saw it ourselves. And even more important than understanding the horror and pain that sin causes, we found ourselves overwhelmed with the love and power of the Almighty.

Truly no one on earth can ever question His love for them or His ability to understand their suffering. How could humans ever doubt their value to the Almighty? Surely just to read His story should make them shout with joy and recognize the huge value He places on them.

And me? I shall continue my recording assignments, though the promises Jesus gave to His disciples excite me too, for surely He will come back for them and we will all live together with Him. Everyone throughout the universe will know that God is love.